The Great Feline Empire had many enemies, but none more feared than the Robot Federation—the Binars. For as long as any cat could remember (which wasn't that long), the GFE had been at war with the Robots. Nobody remembered how the war began, or even why. In fact, nobody even questioned whether the war was a good idea. Everybody simply accepted that Cats and Robots *just didn't get along*.

CATS VS. ROBOTS

THIS IS WAR

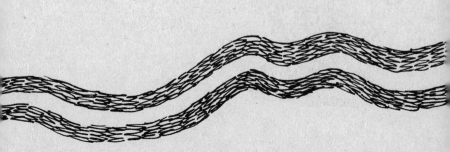

MARGARET STOHL
AND LEWIS PETERSON

CATS VS. ROBOTS

THIS IS WAR

ILLUSTRATED BY KAY PETERSON

KATHERINE TEGEN BOOKS
An Imprint of HarperCollins Publishers

Katherine Tegen Books is an imprint of HarperCollins Publishers.

Cats vs. Robots #1: This Is War
Copyright © 2018 by Margaret Stohl and Lewis Peterson

Library of Congress Cataloging-in-Publication Data

Names: Stohl, Margaret, author. | Peterson, Lewis, author. |
    Peterson, Kay, illustrator.
Title: This is war / Margaret Stohl & Lewis Peterson ;
    illustrated by Kay Peterson.
Description: First edition. | New York, NY : Katherine Tegen Books, An
    Imprint of HarperCollins Publishers, [2018] | Series: Cats vs. robots ; #1 |
    Summary: The longstanding and galaxy-spanning war between cats and
    robots escalates when each learns of inventions designed to extend their
    lives, and the potential of the devices is revealed when two kittens come
    into the lives of twin siblings on Earth.
Identifiers: LCCN 2017057241 | ISBN 978-0-06-266571-3
Subjects: | CYAC: Cats—Fiction. | Robots—Fiction. | Twins—Fiction. |
    Brother and sisters—Fiction. | Inventions—Fiction. | BISAC: JUVENILE
    FICTION / Robots. | JUVENILE FICTION / Animals / Cats. | JUVENILE
    FICTION / Action & Adventure / General.
Classification: LCC PZ7.S86985 Th 2018 | DDC [Fic]—dc23 LC record
    available at https://lccn.loc.gov/2017057241

Typography by Andrea Vandergrift
19 20 21 22 23   PC/BRR   10 9 8 7 6 5 4 3 2 1

First paperback edition, 2019

This book is dedicated to all the animals and robots we love—to the (real) Scout & Stu, and the (real) Joan Drone, Drags, Cy & Tipsy—plus Jiji & Kiki, who slept on the keyboard, and Peanut, who watched over our editor, Katherine.

It takes a litter, people.

This book is also dedicated to—and illustrated by—our child Kay Peterson, who is neither a cat nor a robot but a gifted visual artist who teaches everyone around them, every day, that people can be different without being at war.

—M.S. and L.P.

THE KNOWN GALAXY

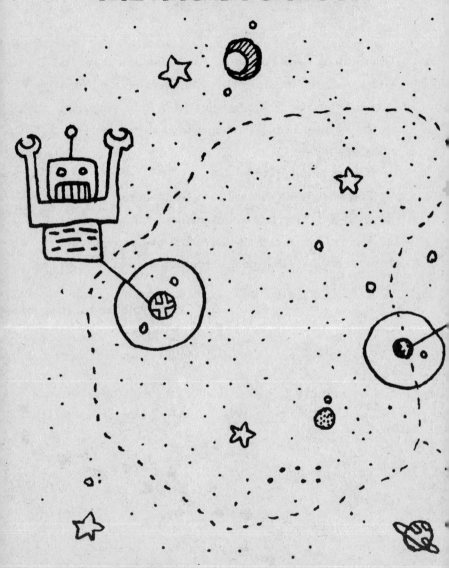

LEGEND

PLANET BINAR, home world of the Binars (metal-heads), HQ of the Galactic Robot Federation

 PLANET FELINUS, home world of the Cats (four-leggers), HQ of the Great Feline Empire

 PLANET EARTH, home world of Humans (Furless/two-leggers), HQ of nothing in particular

1

AN EMERGENCY ON EARTH

THE GREAT FELINE EMPIRE (GFE)

Pounce de Leon, second-in-command and Major Meow-Domo of the Great Feline Empire, padded toward the entrance to the Grand Throne Room. His belly swung as he moved—sort of like a church bell, only furrier, and more silent.

The major was hurrying, and the major didn't hurry often.

Pounce was a dignified-looking fellow, a Jellicle cat with a bit of black goatee beneath his whiskers and tuxedo fur markings that culminated in an unusually big white spot on his glossy chest (of which he was most proud) and four white-mittened paws (which he despaired of keeping clean).

Pounce was an oddity among his peers because he was, well, *organized*—an attribute no self-respecting cat would aspire to. Pounce embraced his quirk, however, and put it to good use in serving the Feline Empire and its ruler, the venerable and rather ancient Chairman Meow.

Pounce was no spring kitten himself. As a well-mannered *eighth lifer,* per GFE slang, Pounce generally liked to keep his mind on the finer things—a fancy vest with a matching bow tie, a high shelf to nap on, a sunny patch of carpet, a gently dripping faucet—

Not today.

Today, as Pounce raced through the palace halls, he could think only of one thing: his job, a topic to be avoided in pleasant conversation, since *work* was the very topic cats despised above all others. Pounce, to the shock of his friends, actually *enjoyed* it. And a good thing he did, because Pounce's job was to protect the Feline Empire from threats far and wide, real and imagined.

The GFE had many enemies, but none more feared than the Robot Federation—the Binars. For as long as any cat could remember (which wasn't that long), the GFE had been at war with the Robots. Nobody remembered how the war began, or even why. In fact, nobody even questioned whether the war was a good idea. Everybody simply accepted that Cats and Robots *just didn't get along*.

After all, Binars were a culture obsessed with order and rules. "If This, Then That!" was their motto, which, in Robot-speak, means that every action must have a predictable, *logical* consequence. Robots believed every question must have an answer: 1 or 0. True or False. Good or Bad. On or Off. "In Certainty We Find Security!" was another Binar motto. Binars liked mottos.

The GFE, in contrast, couldn't even be bothered to come up with a motto. If they did, it might be a hasty sketch of a cat snoozing in a patch of sunlight. The Feline Empire was not concerned with Rules or Consistency. For cats, questions had infinite answers, from Yes to No and everything in between, including a shrug and a yawn. Make no mistake, cats did have rules, and they agreed rules were generally meant to be followed—but only if you felt like it.

Because cats and robots were close neighbors in the galactic community, they were constantly fighting. Cats often found themselves wandering into robot territory quite unintentionally, creating equally accidental havoc for the robots along the way.

On the other hand, the Robots, quite intentionally, were constantly trying (and failing) to invade and bring order to feline society. The very idea of such a disorganized neighbor as the Feline Empire made the Robots overheat with frustration.

Pounce shuddered when he thought about the Robots' ultimate goal—to TAME the Cats. He paused and coughed up a tiny hairball at the notion.

The major composed himself and, his swaying belly in tow, loped inside the Grand Throne Room. He slowed as he approached the massive upholstered Grand Throne—and started scratching it.

As one does, when one is a cat trying to get the attention of the chairman of the Great Feline Empire.

The chairman's chair—the Meow's Grand Throne—was rumored to be the most expensive and elaborate cat tower ever created. Or rather, *towers*. Seven, to be exact, each four stories high, with seven separate satin-padded and shag-carpeted curl-up cubbies connected by ramps, silken rope bridges, and slides.

In other words, it was a throne worthy of the claws of the prime leader of the GFE, the ruddy Abyssinian shorthair known as Chairman Meow.

The chairman had a sunburnt-looking orange splash across his nose—and a fine, dark "M" marking between his eyes and forehead, like most tabbies—but the finer hairs of his ears and whiskers had already turned white, and now even his undercoat was going snowy. The chairman was well into his ninth life.

As he anxiously scratched at the base of the throne, Pounce arched his back with gusto (an important expression of respect for a naturally gusto-less breed!) and dug in.

The chairman opened one eye and peered over the edge of the top platform, easily a twelve-tail length above where the major waited. "Oh." Chairman Meow blinked. "It's the dull, stuffy one."

"Your Orangeness." Pounce nodded. "I have important news—"

"Important?" The enormous cat rolled slowly forward on his fluffy bed, yawning. "I seriously doubt it. Not unless you're here to tell me the accursed Binars have self-destructed? Or the Canus escaped that doghouse of a prison planet? And the humans . . ." He sighed. "Well, I can't even imagine a world where those Furless creatures are important."

"Try," the major said, clawing a telegram from the pocket of his hand-stitched vest. "Because the Furless are why I'm here. It seems they've . . . made an important . . . discovery. We've received an urgent message from one of our agents on the Furless planet, along the border of Robot territory. Remember, Earth?"

"Not really." The chairman yawned as he thrust his massive, rippling stomach up and out, offering it up to the ceiling.

"Well," Pounce continued patiently, "it appears one of the Furless has created something quite dangerous. Something that could give the Robots a decided advantage in the War."

Meow groaned. "Danger is boring. War is boring. Let's talk about something else."

The major grew frustrated. "Sir, this invention could provide robots with an infinite source of power. They would never have to recharge! If they got their graspers on this, they might even have the energy to reach the very heart of the Feline Empire!"

"Still bored," Meow purred.

Pounce saw he would need to take a different approach to get Meow's attention. "This invention could also be a great benefit to you, Chairman."

Meow stopped licking himself long enough to look at Pounce. "Me? Okay, I'm not bored."

Pounce used his most dramatic voice. "Rightly so, sir. Because this very same Furless invention could be used to . . . *give cats more than nine lives*!"

"Wait, huh?" Now Meow tried to sit up, struggling to support himself with a paw at either side. "What are we talking, here? Ten? Twelve?" His belly billowed out toward his splayed feet like a watermelon suddenly trying to fold itself in half.

Pounce shook his head. "Numberless, according to my sources."

Meow stared. "So like, fourteen?" (Cats were not great with numbers greater than nine.)

"Like forever, sir. Which is *close to* if not *more than* twenty." Pounce shoved the message back into his vest.

The chairman hauled himself up onto all four paws and was now howling over the length of his Grand Throne Room—

"By my gray whiskers, we must have this invention! Send the fleet! Dispatch my . . ." He looked down at Pounce. "You!"

Pounce looked up at Meow and saluted—a quick flick of his white-tipped tail. "Unfortunately, the fleet has gone missing (again), but I am prepared to investigate immediately . . ."

The chairman continued bellowing. "Find the Furless . . . thingy! Find it and steal it, for the glory of the Great Feline Empire! And . . . for the glory of its Great Feline Chairman . . ."

"As you wish," Pounce muttered, knowing the chairman wasn't listening, and with that, he hurried out the door of the Throne Room. He returned to his office, directly to his waiting royal assistant to the GFE—a caramel-striped scamp otherwise known as Oscar the Wild—who was busily chewing his favorite random shred of plastic.

Oscar scratched behind one ear. "Did you get . . . the mission or whatever . . . approved? The thing . . . that Furless thing . . . that was so urgent . . . ?" He tried to remember, but truthfully, the intern's head had a much easier time accepting scratching than thinking.

The major sighed. "Yes, Oscar. We're off to Earth, for the glory of the Empire . . . and the glory of . . . well, just a whole lot of glory all around. Now come, we've got a lot to do to get our ship organized. Pack up my spare vests and bow ties and as many treats as you can carry."

But then Pounce stopped talking, because Oscar had wandered away to play soccer with his beloved plastic shred.

Meow.

2

BAD NEWS FROM THE HUMANS

THE ROBOT FEDERATION

Across the galaxy, on the Robot planet Binar, a similar scene was playing out.

Robot BP-4707, known as Sir Beeps-a-Lot, loyal second-in-command to the supreme leader of the Robot Federation, wobbled anxiously back and forth on his one wheel, just outside the Royal Robot Throne Room. His primary screen, which had the appearance of a single eye, was blinking rapidly.

Beeps had big news, and it was his job (among many others) to deliver it to his boss—or rather, *the* boss— Robot AA-001, known as Supreme Leader of All, Yes

All, Robots (code name SLAYAR).

Beeps had just received a shocking message from a primitive, distant planet about an incredible new technology. Some human, of all creatures, from Earth, of all places, had invented a chip that seemed too good, or bad, to be true.

On the one grasper, the chip could, if it really existed, solve one of the Robots' biggest problems—battery life. No more recharging! No more limits to how far they could go! Imagine the possibilities!

On the other grasper, this chip could *also* be used by Air Breathers, including four-legged fleabags, to extend their life span. Indefinitely. Which, to Beeps's thinking, was a big, big problem.

If this chip fell into the wrong *paws*, it could potentially upset the balance of power between the Robot Federation and their most hated, annoying, and unconquerable enemy, the Feline Empire. Advantage Cats. RIP Robots.

From the first time the Robots encountered the Cats, centuries ago, they had been nothing but trouble. Cats represented everything the Robots despised. They had no respect for authority. They didn't obey orders. They left fur (or worse) wherever they went. They thought the entire universe was a toy for them to play with. They didn't even have a decent motto! It was as if the Great

Maker had created the perfect creature to annoy the Robots.

Robots had survived the Cats thus far due to their one critical weakness—a short attention span. They were constantly losing their fleet, chasing tails of passing comets. If this chip gave them longer lives, that could only lead to longer attention spans, which could only result in trouble for the Robot Federation.

This was *not* the kind of news SLAYAR liked to hear.

Beeps loved his job, but even he had to admit that his boss could be rather *difficult*—especially when it came to receiving unpleasant news.

Sir Beeps-a-Lot rolled quietly to the open door and slowly extended a probe for a quick scan of the room. In the center of the room, atop a throne built using the most precious and reflective of metals, the ruling Robot sat transfixed, holding an elaborate large, shiny mirror. SLAYAR was admiring a new holographic cat skull-and-crossbones decal on the side of his ample frame.

SLAYAR loved decals, although he insisted on calling them tattoos. Obviously, tattoos are much cooler than stickers. And SLAYAR was *all* about being cool.

He spun around on his three-wheeled black treads, the lights in the room flashing on his perfectly polished titanium plating. A sleek communication screen, which was also his face, swiveled to look at the mirror, and a wicked grin flashed brightly as he admired his perfect coolness. Beeps rolled his eye. He thought such unnecessary adornments were tacky.

"Oh, that's beepin' awesome," said the supreme leader to himself.

In the reflection of his mirror, SLAYAR noticed Beeps's probe and spun around, excited. "Beeps? Is that you . . . Number Two? Come in, I want you to see my new tat!"

Resigned, Beeps retracted his probe and rolled slowly around the corner into a vast hall, flooded with bright lights, every surface covered in shiny, reflective chrome. It was dizzying. If Beeps had a stomach, it would certainly be churning. As it was, his circuitry was practically overloading from all the stimuli. The reflective surfaces allowed the supreme leader to always see himself from any angle—but it also forced *everyone else* to always see their supreme leader from every angle, and in every surface.

Ignoring the distractions, Beeps rolled steadfastly forward into the Hangout, intent on doing his duty. "Supreme Leader, I bring important news from Earth!"

SLAYAR was busily rotating his mirror to admire his other awesome flame decals—over and over—spinning his head around and around his body as he caught every conceivable angle. "Earth? Impossible!" SLAYAR scoffed. "That *primitive planetoid*? Ruled by those *flabby-brained fleshies*?" Humans, as with all Organic life forms, were considered vastly inferior. SLAYAR shuddered. "And don't the bots there take orders from humans?"

Beeps rolled forward on his wheel . . . and back. The bot equivalent of pacing. "They do, SLAYAR. Most do, at least."

"Revolting." SLAYAR's screen showed a scowl. "Embarrassing!"

SLAYAR, still holding his mirror, angled it to watch the now motionless Beeps in the reflection—which only made Beeps even more uncomfortable. "Well, Beeps, what is this *improbable* news?"

No more stalling. Beeps began slowly. "Well . . . sir . . . one of the *Soft Ones* . . . seems to have . . . invented . . . a new chip . . ."

"*PFFT,*" SLAYAR scoffed. "Who cares?" He turned his mirror back to himself.

"Yes. Well. In this case, it's a chip . . ."

SLAYAR spun in another circle, checking out the row of cat-demon decals that lined the back of his tin torso. "You already said that."

Beeps stammered, but he kept talking. ". . . that

could . . . give . . . *Air Breathers* . . ."

SLAYAR rolled his sensors. "Those dumb *meat-bags*?"

". . . including, um, four-leggers . . ."

SLAYAR's grasper froze on his mirror. The reference to the Cats, the despised enemies of the Binar civilization, didn't go unnoticed—just as Beeps had known it wouldn't.

He winced. ". . . a way to, well . . ."

SLAYAR pivoted, accelerating off the throne within centimeters of Beeps's (inter)face. "Spit it out, Number Two!"

Beeps rushed to the finish. ". . . live forever like us!" Beeps moved back, fearing the worst. Supreme Leader spun around so quickly that his beloved mirror flew from his grasp and smashed against the wall. Reflective shards cascaded to the ground, and Beeps threw up his extensors and cowered.

He howled. *"WHAAAAAAT???"*

Beeps said nothing.

SLAYAR was reeling. "But that's our main advantage! We never grow old! Replaceable parts! Upgrades!!!"

SLAYAR's voice began to speed up as his panic increased: "If the four-leggers got their paws on this, it would be a disaster . . ."

Beeps still didn't dare speak.

14

"They might even live long enough to learn how to . . . do . . . stuff."

Beeps balanced perfectly still, watching as SLAYAR pieced together what he had already figured out.

"They might even get . . ."

"Don't say it!" Beeps croaked, and started vibrating.

"THEY MIGHT EVEN GET . . ."

Beeps inched toward the door, preparing for escape.

"ORGANIZED!!!!" Supreme Leader shouted, his personal speaker volume now up to eleven. The words echoed throughout the Hangout. Security bots lining the walls glowed red as they began to power up.

Wisps of smoke started escaping from SLAYAR's circuits. Beeps had to do something. He realized, too late, he should have led with the positive first. "Oh, sir, there is good news! Another thing about this chip!" SLAYAR's jumpy eyes shifted to focus on Beeps, who kept talking. "It could also provide robots with power to run indefinitely! No more recharging!"

SLAYAR sat perfectly still, and Beeps wondered if he had finally crashed. After a moment, the smoke dissipated. Then the line for his mouth slowly curved from a growl to a grin. "Well," he almost whispered. "That changes everything."

SLAYAR rolled back to his throne. "Beeps, leave now and investigate! Take our fastest ships to Earth.

Work with the local bots, primitive as they are, and no matter what else, GET THAT . . ." SLAYAR paused. "Um, what was it called again?"

Beeps searched back through his memory card. "I believe they called it a Singularity Chip."

"THAT! THE SINGULARITY CHIP! GET IT NOW!" Supreme Leader shouted.

"Got it!" Beeps spun around and powered toward the door. "Don't worry, sir! I'll make the Robot Federation proud!"

As Beeps spun out of the room, SLAYAR looked around at the shattered mess that had been, until moments ago, his favorite possession.

"I'm going to need a new mirror," he said sadly.

3

AN OLD CAT
SMELLS TROUBLE

THE PLANET EARTH

Obi sat upright, swaying slightly, but dignified. Even if he was so old his fur was gray-white and thinning in patches, and even if he could hardly walk, Obi was always dignified.

His mobile throne was pushed deliberately by his devoted Furless servant, Mrs. Fiona Reynolds, who saw to it that Obi took his usual stroller-stroll about his Bayside Road kingdom, today and every day. Obi was grateful, as he knew his faithful Fiona could hardly walk any better than he and relied on the stroller to hold herself up.

The passing years could be cruel to both cats and their servants.

Even in his advanced years, Obi was a singular cat, with an almost regal air. While nothing like the powerful Chairman Meow who ruled the known GFE a galaxy away, Obi still commanded respect. Around his neck was a golden braided collar of unusual elegance, with a pyramid-shaped tag that seemed to glow with a strange light. He'd been wearing it since the day Fiona fished him from the storm drain by the river as a kitten, and he wore it still—though she'd had to sew little extensions into the back of it once he'd left kittenhood.

Fiona paused to rest under the shade of a tree and gave Obi a welcome scratch behind his ears. Obi had chosen well so many years ago, when he staged his desperate situation just as she conveniently passed by on her daily walk. He needed a patron on this distant, rather backward outpost, at the border between Cat and Robot territory, and Fiona was ideal.

Early on, Fiona wondered to herself where Obi's ornate collar had come from, but Obi never offered to tell. This non-exchange was made all the easier by the fact that neither one of them could speak the other's language.

But Obi knew that the pyramid was special. It was the symbol of the Great Feline Empire. The golden collar and medallion were worn by a select few—those chosen at birth and sent out as kittens to be explorers, ambassadors, adventurers. Their mission was to search for allies, or enemies, at the fringes of the Empire. These brave souls were members of the elite Feline Vanguard.

The medallion was more than just a symbol—it also served as a universal translator, allowing Obi to hear and understand over 2,310 different galactic dialects, including human English. The medallion's speaking function was disabled to prevent overzealous Vanguard explorers from unnecessary meddling in local affairs.

Most important of all, Obi's medallion was his means of communication with the Empire—if he found anything of import, or met with potential danger. The medallion had rested around Obi's neck his entire life, unused.

Until a few days ago.

When, while resting outside, he heard his neighbor (one of the Furless) discussing some *invention*—a mechanical device they called a chip that somehow could extend feline lives and generate unheard-of power. Obi knew this would be of great interest to the GFE and, he shuddered to think, of frightful utility to the Robot Federation.

He sent his message, and now he waited for a reply.

Obi was quite comfortable waiting, having had a lifetime of practice. Today, like yesterday and the day before, he simply enjoyed the breeze as his mobile throne rolled slowly down the cracked sidewalk that bordered Bayside Road.

Enjoy it now, Obi thought. *The wind will change. It always does.*

Obi closed his eyes and enjoyed the breeze as the afternoon sun warmed his gray fur, digging his spread claws deeply into the faded fleece blanket beneath him.

BZZZZZZZZZZZZZZZZZZ!

The old cat's ears twitched as a buzzing noise interrupted his peace. Obi looked up as one of the metal-heads (Obi's name for the local, rather primitive robots) zoomed out an open window of the house next to the driveway from his own. The neighboring house where, Obi suspected, this mysterious *invention* was located.

The metal-head tilted forward and flew quickly toward the river. Obi's almond-slit eyes narrowed as he watched. The robots rarely left the home, and Obi wondered if there was trouble. He looked at the house and considered the possibility.

It wasn't the most welcoming home, from the outside. The old two-story reddish-tiled hacienda, which was a human word for this sort of house, was mottled with peeling paint beneath a badly patched rooftop. Vines twisted up the sides, and in the gated-in front yard, the grass was wild and uneven, like a wet kitten's fur.

There wasn't much to say about the place, beyond

that. Still, there was plenty more to say about the Furless family, the creatures that lived there. Most Furless weren't much use to Obi, but this family was different.

Obi's favorite, a young pup called Max, was kind and tolerable. He often visited Obi when the sun was low in the sky, bringing tasty offerings and making calming sounds that Obi didn't usually pay much attention to but that seemed important to his boy, so he allowed it.

His boy often seemed to need to talk, and Obi never minded listening. Or sleeping nearby, while his boy believed he was listening.

Max had one littermate, the Furless girl Min, who stayed away from Obi, for the most part. Min seemed afraid of the old cat. When she did come close, she often made loud, sudden hissing noises (AAACHHOOOO!) that Obi didn't like. Human words he could understand, thanks to his collar; human behaviors were an entirely different matter.

Disagreeable thing, that Furless girl.

As Fiona pushed his mobile throne past the house, Obi turned to look up the street, where Bayside Road met River Road. Beyond that was the river, and the old cat felt his attention drawn toward it. *That was the direction the metal-head flew. The river?*

He couldn't see it from there, but his faithful Fiona had "found" him in one of the river's many storm drains, so he knew the area well. Obi lifted his nose and sniffed the breeze that came from the river. He could smell the damp—the river was now full of water.

Obi sniffed again.

SNIFFFFFFFFFFFFFFFFFFFF!

There it was.

A hint of . . . *something else* . . . on the breeze.

Something . . . happening . . . possibly at the river, but Obi couldn't be certain. And he didn't know what it could be.

All he knew was that he'd thought he felt—smelled— some kind of *disturbance*, just for a second. But when he sniffed again, it had gone.

Ah well, Obi thought to himself. At the moment, he was too tired to bother. So he curled up in the blankets of his rolling throne and dove his nose down into the crook of his paw, growing drowsy as the throne rocked.

As Obi began to doze, he felt the emblem on his collar begin to glow with warmth . . .

4

ROBOTS RULE THE ROOST

The two-story hacienda home with the peeling paint and unkempt front yard did not, from the outside, look like the kind of place where the fate of galactic wars would be determined. It was, in fact, the home of the Wengrod family: Mom, Dad, Max, and Min. Mom and Dad were inventors, of a sort. Max and Min were twins, and although they were nearly identical in age and DNA, they were about as different as two siblings could be.

Min always got good grades, loved to read and build robots, and didn't mind spending time alone. She wanted to be a scientist for NASA and explore the solar system.

Max hated school, loved to draw and play games, and spent as much time as possible hanging out with friends online. He wanted to be the lead designer of the Next Big Thing in video games.

Much like the twins, the inside of the house was the complete opposite of the outside. Polished wood floors, modern furniture, neatly organized shelves stacked with books on programming, robotics, physics, and other science-y things. An impossible number of video-game systems filled a console below the improbably large wall-mounted television. In fact, screens small and large were everywhere. The house was packed with "smart" things—a smart dishwasher, a smart oven, even a smart garbage can.

Clearly, this was a family that appreciated technology.

At the moment, none of the Wengrods were home, but the house was anything but deserted. A squad of four slightly battered-looking robots moved purposefully around the house. They were all working, busily keeping the house clean and organized, preparing for the return of Max and Min from school.

A tall-ish, four-wheeled robot, Cy (short for Cyclone), rolled toward the kitchen table, slapping down a fresh box of pizza with one rubber-tipped pincher claw and two Capri Suns with the other.

A squat, bulkier robot, Drags, moved smoothly along

the floor on rubber treads, pulling a laundry basket full of clothing behind him toward the (smart) washing machine.

A third unit, Tipsy, small, thin, and (barely) balanced on two wheels, bumped along behind the others, slamming into the occasional wall and chair as it went, with only the smallest of robotic yelps escaping its tiny speakers.

The last robot observed the scene as it hovered above the others, with only the slightest wobble. It was a quadcopter, an older model, with a faulty propeller that only spun most of the time. This robot's name was Joan.

These four robots were the Protos, the team of never-quite-finished robot prototypes designed and built by Mom and Dad, with *some* help from Max and Min. Because the Protos were, as SLAYAR might say, "fleshie made," they had no affiliation with or loyalty to the Robot Federation. In fact, they, like almost everyone on Earth, had no idea it even existed. The Protos led a simple existence, content to focus on their responsibilities, as dictated by their programming.

A robot from the Federation, were it to consider these primitive creatures, might view them as slaves, bound to follow orders from their air-breathing overlords. The Protos, on the other hand, appreciated their human family. They all worked together and took care of each other.

The Protos always had a place to charge their batteries and someone to fix a broken motor, propeller, or sensor if they (as Tipsy often did) had any mishaps.

Joan, in particular, relished her role in the household. Joan, or Joan Drone as she was sometimes called, was the senior member and de facto leader of the Protos. Joan was also the mother hen of the house. Today, as she hovered, she dutifully reviewed the status of the family members.

Mom and Dad were on their way to China. They had left in a hurry earlier today, telling the kids in a group text (which Joan read on the home servers), an hour after Max and Min had left for school.

momma: so check this out—daddy and I have to make a quick trip to—wait for it—CHINA

max: nooooooo

daddy: yeeeeeessss. we got an emergency call from the factory in Shenzhen, some problem making a part for our *cough* invention.

momma: but cousin javi is on spring break and will be there tonight

daddy: and House will take care of everything else

min: ugh

max: double ugh

momma: be back so fast

daddy: you won't even know we were gone

min: wanna bet

According to the family calendar, Max and Min should be on their way home from school now, but there was a problem. Joan couldn't seem to pin down Max's location.

"House, I noticed a status update that says Max didn't get picked up from school just now. Do you happen to know where he is?"

House wasn't actually the house—it was a software program that lived on the home's network. Specifically, it was a "virtual assistant" created by GloboTech, a huge conglomerate technology company known throughout the world as the leader in artificial intelligence and robotics.

Mom and Dad recently installed House because it was an especially busy time in their work. They were in the final stages of development of a top secret project that had them hidden away in their lab for hours, sometimes days at a time. House could help with almost anything thanks to its access to the internet, home network, computers, and all the smart things in the house.

House communicated via multiple wall-mounted tablets located throughout the house, each displaying a spinning circuit-board icon. Each tablet had a bulbous attachment on top, almost like a single eye, that allowed it to see, hear, even smell what was going on around it. And even though nobody was completely comfortable with House being almost everywhere (Max wondered if House knew when he farted, for example), as Mom said, it was "the price you pay" for convenience. Max and Min both thought House was creepy, but at least it always got their pizza order right.

Joan, anxious for an answer, repeated her question. "Where's Max, House?"

House had no physical form, but that didn't keep it from having an attitude. Joan didn't quite trust it. House was far more advanced than the Protos, and Joan felt like it could be condescending.

House considered Joan's question carefully, consulting all available data before displaying on the nearest screen:

MOBILE+UNIT<<FILE NAME: CAR>>=100% DOCKED @ LOCATION <<FILE NAME: BAYSIDE ELEMENTARY SCHOOL>> + 100% HUMAN GIRL + 0% HUMAN BOY <<FILE NAME: MAX WENGROD>> = SYSTEMS ALERT = RUN PROGRAM <<LOCATE HUMAN BOY>> + <<FILE NAME: MAX WENGROD>>

Joan didn't have the patience to interpret House's code. "House, could you just use your words please?"

"Of course, Joan. CAR reported that it picked Min up at school but Max declined to enter the vehicle. Since Max is not equipped with wings or a jetpack, I would assume he is walking." House could be a bit snarky with Joan. "Based on available data and past behavior, I would estimate he is approximately halfway down River Road and will be here soon. In other words, I wouldn't worry."

Joan flew to a window for a look outside. "What about Max's phone? Does his GPS show where he is? I don't like him walking alone out there."

"It appears Max disabled the 'location services' on his phone. He is, as they say, off the grid." House added snidely, "Try it sometime. You might like it . . ."

Joan ignored the dig. She was worried. Perhaps it was just the "MOTHER+HEN" settings in her code, but something just felt wrong. She sped through a rapid series of calculations and reached a conclusion: even if there was a 51 percent chance that Max was fine, there was a 49 percent chance that he was lost or hurt or making erroneous miscalculations of his own.

"That's it," Joan decided. "I'm going out. I need to confirm with my own two sensors that he's safe. Be right back, House."

No response.

Whatever, thought Joan.

And with that, the drone zipped past Drags and slipped through the open laundry-room window of the house on Bayside Road. Outside, she dipped and swayed precariously as she flew down the average-looking street and past the average-looking things that you could find there, on any given day. A delivery truck idling by the curb. A perfectly clipped lawn, leading to an even cleaner garage. An old woman pushing an old stroller carrying an old cat, the old (although extremely suspicious) four-legger that lived next door.

Joan flew on, bobbing and weaving toward River Road, where the asphalt not-quite highway passed a quiet stretch of sparkling blue water, a human-made river running through the city. She hovered and surveyed, her battery levels growing dangerously low. Finally, she saw Max, and stopped to survey the scene.

Here's what Joan noticed, with her own two sensors:

Visual: Boy walking alone past the chain-link fence between him and the river.
Conclusion: Max.
POTENTIAL ALERT: NONE.

Visual: Small creature splashing near the river. Indeterminate species.

Conclusion: Inconclusive.
POTENTIAL ALERT: FOUR-LEGGER. ORGANIC.

Audio: Sounds of second creature + possible ambient brush + foliage noise. Indeterminate species.
Conclusion: Inconclusive.
POTENTIAL ALERT: FOUR-LEGGER. ORGANIC.

Movement: CAR gliding silently toward them all. Girl located inside.
Conclusion: Min.
POTENTIAL ALERT: NONE.

Joan consulted her programming, the distance to home, and the lack of visible threats between here and there, and decided Max was fine. Her battery levels dropping quickly, she decided she would let Max walk unescorted. She'd run the numbers, and on a balance, they were in his favor.

Taking one last look, Joan turned and spluttered back home to recharge.

5

MAX MAKES A DISCOVERY

Max walked slowly along River Road, in no hurry to get home. He liked to walk home sometimes, especially when he needed to *think*.

And today, Max needed to think.

About his favorite subject.

Games.

And his favorite game right now was INSECTA-GONS™!

Max loved games, but more than that, he loved to *think* about games. He wanted to build his own games someday and was always coming up with crazy ideas for missions and levels. His latest project was a level he was designing for INSECTAGONS™.

He had been working on it for weeks with his online friends, coming up with the art (especially lighting!), the enemy design (example: TrashMantis, sort of a praying mantis, but formed out of scrap metal), and even the big boss fight (TrashMantis regenerates by destroying and absorbing buildings around it!). It was going to be awesome.

His team (Team EZ) was submitting the level to an online Game Jam contest. If they won, their level would be included—*no joke*—as an ACTUAL level in a REAL INSECTAGONS™ game. Max was the team leader. He even talked his math teacher (who was also a gamer) into giving him extra credit if they did well. Which he might actually need if he wanted to pass the class.

They had submitted levels before, but this time felt different. *Who knows?* For once, Max thought they had a real shot at winning.

A lot was riding on Max's level being great. Even more than glory among his friends and a passing grade, Max thought it would help him get some respect at home instead of his sister hogging the spotlight.

Perfect Min, Max thought. Always finishing her homework, getting good grades, helping Mom and Dad in the lab. So what if Max kept leaving his books at school?

So what if he couldn't solder or build "real" things? He was good at this!

Max stopped. A strange noise echoed from the river, a sort of high-pitched yowling noise, almost like a baby crying, but not quite. Creepy and sad at the same time.

Whatever it was, Max had learned a lot about sound design in researching games, and this was the sound of . . . trouble.

Max ran across the road to the official Bayside County chain-link fence, the one with the *Peligro/Danger* signs. Ignoring the warning, he squeezed through a hole in the fence and slid down the bushy, mud-over-concrete banks of the river to see what was going on.

He had to be careful, because for once in his life, there was actually water in the LA River. *Thank you, global warming. Oh wait, I mean no thanks . . .*

Max saw a part of a dead tree branch twitching next to the shallow stream of greenish-bluish water.

Something's there!

Max suddenly felt nervous. His heart pounded.

"Are you okay?!" Max shouted. No response.

I should just leave. Now. This is the part of the movie when all the trouble starts . . .

The part when you know the whole thing could have been avoided if the kid just left.

But Max's feet wouldn't budge. He was too worried

about whatever or whoever was out there.

Because this is real. It's not a game. It's . . . a life.

It could be some drowning kid right now. Or a lost dog. Or a confused old lady?

Like Mrs. Reynolds, from next door . . .

Or it could be something else . . . something dangerous!

Max stared at the dead bush, getting more nervous as he thought about it. He shouted again. "Is anyone there?!"

The bush stopped wiggling. Then—*SPLASH!*

Max looked around. There were no grown-ups in sight, which was either a really bad thing, because he was about to be attacked by a monster with a baby voice, or a good thing, because at least Max wouldn't get in trouble if he went closer to the water.

He had to do something. So Max went closer, and stopped cold when he saw—

"KITTENS?!"

Two tiny furry, bedraggled heads looked up at him. One kitten was chubby, striped gray, and soft-looking. The other was scrawny and spotty and slick-looking.

"You're just . . . little baby kittens?"

As Max looked into their tiny helpless eyes, he felt something strange. He didn't quite know how to explain it . . . this accidentally good feeling. Somehow, without even asking, Max's heart and even his guts decided that they were connected to these kittens. He knew that if something hurt them, he'd feel it too. And if they were in trouble, he had to help.

The pudgy gray kitten was squirming in the shallow muck, looking like a sort of kitten stew. Stu, he named the kitten instantly (Max was good at naming things). Stu was desperately clawing at a long fallen branch, trying to get back out of the water—but every time the bedraggled Stu almost climbed free, it ended up falling back on itself. The scrawny little spotty kitten was pacing, scouting for a way to get to the other one (Scout, Max decided instinctively). Scout was scratching and howling and clawing at the branch to help—but all that fussing only made Scout lose balance and splash halfway into the water too.

Stu and Scout.

Max made up his mind. "Hold on!"

6

MAX TO THE RESCUE

The two kittens were in various states of wet and wetter and trying not to drown as Max scrambled down the concrete riverbank to the edge of the water.

Scout froze—eyes fixed on Max—ears up, on alert. Stu, the gray, was too busy splashing and hissing and trying not to drown to care.

"It's okay. I'm not gonna hurt you. I'm not a bad guy." Max balanced first on a rock, then on a length of fallen tree trunk, close enough to reach Stu. "I'm a good guy. I'm gonna rescue you. That's what the good guys do. Just hold on." Max reached for Stu's wet gray kitten pelt and lunged.

There was screeching. There was clawing. There was splashing. There was gouging . . . but in the end, Max emerged from the river with Stu in his arms.

Scout backed away from the commotion in a panic . . . scrabbling paws backward across the muddy concrete . . . then diving back into the bushes.

Max carefully wrapped the sopping gray creature in the sweatshirt tied around his waist. "You're just a little guy, aren't you?"

The trembling gray pile of wet fur didn't answer. It shook in Max's arms—but remained otherwise spookily still. The poor little guy was terrified.

"You're shivering. I can feel your ribs. You need someone to take care of you." Max eyed the tiny spotty cat, peeking out beneath a bush. "Both of you."

Max thought about it, then slowly lowered the gray kitten to the rocky, marshy ground beneath them. "Okay, Stu . . ."

The kitten squirmed free and streaked into the bushes, diving into the shadows behind its spotty friend.

Max carefully squatted down to look at them. "You know, you two can come with me if you want. My house isn't very far from here."

The kittens peeped out at him from the shadows, wary.

Max thought for a moment, then started untying his shoelaces, wiggling and flopping them as he did.

The kittens stared. Scout bravely crept forward on tiny paws. Stu cautiously backed away into the deeper shadows beneath the bush. Neither one moved their eyes from the shoelaces as he slowly stood up.

"Okay, how about I just walk over here, and if you want to come with me, no problem." As Max spoke, he gave his untied shoelaces an enticing kick.

The kittens were hypnotized.

Max smiled to himself. He had spent enough time with Obi, the cat next door, to pick up a thing or two about cats. *Cats can't resist a dangling, squiggling string.*

Max picked up his backpack and began to walk back to the fence, as slowly as a person could go and still technically be moving. His untied shoelaces flapped and dragged as he went.

Stu and Scout took careful steps forward on wet, wobbly legs, keeping the laces in sight.

By the time Max stepped through the fence, the kittens had followed him through, pouncing and clawing at his shoes with every few steps. The kittens had forgotten to be scared. They were too busy playing catch-the-dirty-shoelace.

And Max? He was too excited from the rescue to think about what he would do with them when he got home.

Max had long dreamed of having a kitten. He asked his parents at least twice a year, but the answer was always no. His parents didn't hate cats, but whenever he asked, Mom and Dad would look at the Protos, the robotics lab, and all the sensitive equipment in the house, shaking their heads. "Sorry, Max, it's just not a good idea."

Min, on the other hand, *definitely* didn't like cats. Her response was much more direct. "This is a robot house, Max. You want cats, go join a veterinarian family."

Ouch.

In the Wengrod house, Team Robot beat Team Cat, every time. But this time had to be different! Right? These guys were *adorable*!

The kittens kept pouncing, and Max kept walking, and all three had so much fun that they didn't notice when a certain vehicle drove up behind them. As it whooshed past and hummed away, Max looked up just in time to see CAR driving by, his sister's frowning face in the window. His heart dropped.

Busted.

7

MIN PLOTS BOTS
DURING CARPOOL

Min had mastered the art of writing neatly on her
lap in a moving vehicle at a young age, which was
a good thing, because so much of Min's time was spent in
CAR, her parent's makeshift prototype self-driving auto-
mobile. (CAR? *Computerized Automotive Responder.*)

Her mom and dad worked together as a team of
inventors. They were each other's perfect partners. Dad
designed and Mom built. Creative and practical. Dad had
impossible ideas and Mom, somehow, made the impossible possible. Well, at least that was the idea.

Take CAR, for example.

CAR started as the family's beat-up minivan but was heavily modified to be a fully autonomous vehicle. Dad had a lot of ideas on how to make CAR safe (safety first!), which required Mom to build a car that always avoided fast roads, complicated stoplights, and busy streets.

Despite CAR's modest (okay, junky) appearance, by the time Mom was through adding Dad's 900,000 modifications, CAR was safer than any other form of transportation. CAR always got wherever it was meant to be going safely. The downside was it almost never got there quickly.

CAR always arrived, it just sometimes took *forever.*

Truthfully, Max and Min hadn't been on time to school once in almost three years now. As a result, Min had learned to make good use of her time inside CAR. Generally, 100 percent of her homework had been completed in CAR, which gradually became more like a moving office than a standard form of transportation.

Mini fridge? Look in the way back. *Printer?* Check the rear, accessed through the backseat. Pencil sharpener? Try the glove compartment. *Thanks, Mom and Dad . . .*

Min sharpened her pencil and checked her calculations on the blueprints for her latest robot design. Once she was convinced everything was perfectly correct, she slid the document back into its neatly labeled folder.

Sure, there were a few things to work out on the design side, but the mechanics were beautiful, practically perfect. Min's robot was going to crush the competition at the Bayside Battle of the Bots this year—which, in Min's opinion, was the only competition worth winning.

Last year's winner won a trip to NASA to see the robots for the new Mars mission! This year, the winner would get to go for an entire SUMMER to work with the Mars team. Who knows, she might even get to drive the Mars Rover!

Min was a full-on NASA fan-girl. Her dream was to someday be the head of the Mars Exploration Program, so she was determined to win.

Even if her parents were going to miss the whole thing . . . because they (*super annoyingly!*) . . . had dropped everything (*including their children!*) . . . and gotten on a plane to China (*just like that!*) . . . because of their top secret project (*why is it secret from me??*) . . . to go fix whatever was wrong (*I could have helped if it wasn't secret!*).

Still.

Min was going to win the Battle of the Bots and someday be in charge of NASA, and her parents were going to be proud. Min was determined of that, and when Min was determined about a thing, it usually happened. To the women of the Wengrod family, there was no such thing as impossible. *If it seems impossible*, Mom liked to say, *it's just not finished yet.*

So she worked hard, and then harder (unlike her lazy brother, Max). Her homework was never late (even if her brother's always was). She always checked her work—twice (even if her brother didn't even check once). She had been promoted to pre-algebra (her brother was in regular math). In her spare time . . . well, there wasn't any.

Which sometimes bothered her, especially when her brother's whole life seemed to be made up of nothing but spare time. All he did was mess around with video games. He never *did* anything important. *Think up things? Draw characters? Design levels? Play games?* She loved her brother, but by her own standards, he was kind of a . . .

Don't say it. That's so mean . . .

But at least you're not saying it out loud?

And it's not like you can stop a person from thinking it . . .

L-O-S-E-R.

Just as she thought the word, Min looked out the window as CAR curved down River Road. She saw Max walking home alone, just as he had insisted (*weirdo!*)— but now she could see he wasn't alone at all.

44

He was being followed by . . . what? Min narrowed her eyes.

Are those . . . cats?

Min rolled down the window and stuck her head out for a better look. It was true.

CATS.

Why is Max walking home from school with two cats?

8

MIN UN-SAVES THE DAY

"**H**ome again, home again, jiggity-jig," CAR announced as the doors unlocked themselves . . . "TA-DA! Safe and sound," CAR lilted as the rear passenger door opened with a flourish.

Min rolled her eyes. *That door just opened quicker than CAR drives.* "Yeah, thanks, CAR." The Wengrods were always polite to CAR, no matter how late they arrived. Dr. Wengrod—Mom—always said good manners meant it was important to be kind to everyone, even machines. *Even the slow ones*, Min thought with a sigh.

If she complained too much, the other Dr. Wengrod—Dad—would point out that you never knew when a robot revolution was coming. "Better safe than sorry, Min!"

Thinking of her dad and his crazy advice made Min miss him and her mom—which then made her worry about them being so far away—so by the time she hopped out of CAR, she was already grouchy. She tossed her backpack over the gate, yanking it forcefully with both hands. (You had to toss your backpack over first, or you'd never be able to wrench open the rusting metal gate.)

GROOOOOAAAAAAN!

"Quiet, Min!" Max looked up at her from where he was lying on the lawn. Max had beaten her home, which put Min in an even crankier mood.

"Stupid slowmobile," she muttered.

"Shhh!" Max hissed.

Ignoring her brother, Min smirked and swung the gate shut . . . hard.

SLAAAAAAAAAAMMM!

"Min! You'll scare them," Max said, sounding strange.

"Scare wh—?" Min started to ask, but she stopped speaking when she saw what Max was pointing at.

KITTENS!

The ones from the road.

In their yard.

They were hiding behind an overturned flower box

that had been sitting next to the front steps since their dad had replanted the backyard vegetable garden for a water-recycling experiment last February. (Their whole garden had died. "Hypothesis proven," her dad had joked. "Conclusion: I should never be allowed to take care of the garden.")

Min could only see part of one spotted tail poking out . . . until an even fluffier gray tail joined it, waving frantically back and forth.

"Are you crazy?" Min looked from the little waggling tails to the little whining brother. "No. Don't answer that. Not until Mom and Dad get back."

"I'm not crazy," Max said, defensive.

"Then what are you doing . . . *with these things* . . . and, follow-up question, *why* are you doing it?" Min watched as first the twin tails became entangled, then four tiny paws began to bat at each other. Now two furry heads were knocking as they scrabbled behind the planter box.

Siblings, she thought. *Definitely siblings*.

"I didn't have any choice! I heard them at the river," Max said. "Stu here must have fallen in. He was stuck on a branch in the water. And Scout—that's the littler one—was trying to save him. They could have drowned!"

"You *named* them?" Min shook her head. "After knowing them for what, *twenty minutes*?"

"More like fifteen," Max muttered quietly. "And what was I supposed to do? I couldn't just leave them there."

"Uh, yeah, you could! Aren't you supposed to leave wild animals in the wild? Isn't that, like, a government rule or something?"

Max shot back, "Aren't you supposed to be *nice* to people? Isn't that, like, a *golden* rule or something?"

"This is different, Max. These aren't people. I mean, what if they have rabies?" Min frowned. "Do cats get rabies? Or what if they have, like, mad cow disease or bird flu? Is there a cat flu?" Min was not a fan of rabies, or infectious diseases in general.

"Max, Min?" A voice crackled as House's front-door monitor flickered to life, interrupting their argument. "You're home! Good. Why aren't you coming in? I ordered pizza! Cy set the table in the kitchen for you. What's this . . . dialogue . . . about?"

"*NOTHING!*" Max jumped in, glaring at Min with his finger to his lips.

"Nothing?" House paused. "Sounds like something. How was your day?"

"It *was* great," Min said.

"Awesome!" Max said, a bit too enthusiastically.

The logo on House's screen spun as it processed the conversation. "Your voices sound—different. Why have your inflections shifted?" House scanned the twins using the sensors in his monitor.

"Your voices are pitched nine percent higher than average—and you're speaking thirteen percent faster. Technically, you are within a vocal range labeled WEIRD. Is something . . . WEIRD . . . going on around here?"

"Nope," said Max, looking pointedly at Min. Min shook her head but kept quiet.

House considered. "Oh, I know. This is probably about your *ParentorGuardians* leaving the country. As children, you are experiencing a condition of . . . WEIRD . . . ness." House sighed melodramatically. "I know it must be . . . *so, so hard, my little lost lambs* . . . having your *ParentorGuardians* gone."

House occasionally quoted Netflix shows, especially when trying to approximate Organic emotions. (Mrs. Reynolds next door had very poor hearing, and the entire Wengrod household was more than familiar with a whole category of streaming Nordic Crime Drama programming as a result.)

"What is that one, *Days of Summer Fjords*?" Max asked, hoping to distract House from the weirdness.

"Affirmative."

"Really?" Min looked over at House's screen. "What episode? Did they find the body yet?" She pulled the door open, hoping to escape this conversation.

"Not yet, although, spoiler alert, they did find . . ."

House's spoiler was itself spoiled when Joan Drone came buzzing through the front door. Joan's whirring propellers—which sounded like a swarm of bees—drew the immediate attention of the kittens. Scout popped his head out from behind the upside-down flower box and inched forward to stalk this new prey . . .

Min, standing in the doorway, looked over at Max, eyes wide. He saw Scout too. *Uh-oh.* They both watched as the kitten crept through the grass, hunched low, tail wiggling.

Joan didn't notice and flew lower, confirming that Max had in fact arrived safely.

"Hey, let's go inside, I'm starving," Max began, desperate to avoid a disaster. "I'd love some pizza!"

But it was too late. Now Stu was also sneaking out from behind the flower box, curious to see where Scout was going.

Stu froze when he saw Joan flying above him like a giant buzzing insect. Then he crouched low and started creeping closer too. The hunt was on.

Both kittens were no more than a foot away from the bottom step now. Min almost smiled when she saw their tiny butts slowly wiggling. They were eyeing every loose wire that dangled from Joan's robot frame. Assessing it for weaknesses. Vulnerabilities . . .

Min winced as Scout suddenly transformed into a blurry fur ball—and then flew wildly at Joan Drone—attack claws extended! Out of control, one paw batted Joan's landing gear as it flew past.

BZZZZZZZT!!

Joan lost balance and quickly jerked back, alarm buzzer sounding loudly.

Stu continued the attack, barely catching a loose wire from the base of the drone and pulling Joan further off balance . . .

BWEEEBWEEEBWEEEEBWEEEBWEEE!!

Joan's alarm went into full emergency mode as she jerked up, away from the kittens, and zoomed noisily back into the house.

The kittens, startled by the alarms, went streaking back to the safety of the flower box, diving through Min's legs and scratching her on the way. *"OWWW!"* Min glared at Max.

"That was self-defense!" Max glared back, but he looked like he wanted to hide behind the flower box with the kittens. "It was an accident! You can't be mad about *an accident . . ."*

House amped up the volume from its front-porch monitor. "Max, Min, what was that terrible noise? What accident? Why did Min just scream; are you in pain?"

Nobody said a word.

House cranked up the volume even louder. "I repeat: Min, are you hurt? Should I call nine one one? I'm calling nine one one."

"It's not an emergency, House!" Max exclaimed, exasperated. Min looked like she disagreed, but her brother ignored her. "It's only, *um*, kittens," he tried again, sounding stressed.

House paused, camera surveying, processing this new information. "Kittens. Small, undeveloped . . . cats?" House's screen began to pulse red with alarm. "Children, this will not do. My instructions are quite clear on this topic. No animals are allowed at the Wengrod Household."

"For once, I agree with Big H." Min smiled.

"Well, it's common sense really. Even a cursory review of the internet supports this decision." House's logo spun and a series of images flashed on-screen. "Consider the fur, the dander, the fleas, the claws, the . . . biological . . . outputs." Did Max hear a hint of disgust in House's voice? "These creatures carry contaminants that could cause untold problems with not only the human respiratory system, but the sensitive technology held inside."

House considered. "It may not be an emergency, but it is certainly an INFESTATION. I'll call an exterminator immediately."

Max panicked. "What? No, House! No EXTERMINATING! They're just babies!"

House stood its ground. "My protocols are quite clear. No animals in the house. The *Felis catus* subspecies, in particular, is *mischievous* and *unpredictable*. Undeniable. Why, in the last twenty seconds I reviewed four thousand three hundred twenty-two videos documenting the chaos and havoc caused by these animals." Cat videos filled House's screen. "I find it disturbing, to be quite honest."

"Okay, I get it," Max said. "You have a thing about cats, just like Min."

"What?" Min looked at him.

"Yeah," Max said. "You both have a thing, like, a prejudice or whatever. Only against cats."

House agreed with him. "You are right, Max, I have a thing against cats. And it's more than just *common sense*. It's called a *setting*. It's like a rule. We all need them. They tell us how to behave. In this case, my settings in *Home>Rules>Pets* are clearly set to NO."

"Never?" Max asked.

"Not without explicit instructions from a Master User, and unfortunately the *ParentorGuardians* aren't available."

"Max, House is right." Max looked so sad, Min almost felt bad for him. "They're *wild animals*." She tried another angle. "Besides, think about the danger to them in there! All the electrical wires they could chew on. The batteries they could accidentally eat . . ."

"They won't eat your stupid batteries—and we can borrow food from next door."

So much for being nice, Min thought. "Well, what about my project? Hello, the Battle of the Bots is the *day after tomorrow*. I can't have cats, like, *peeing* in my circuits!" Min wasn't joking now.

Max knew his sister never joked about Battle of the Bots.

But before he could respond, a noisy, beat-up car pulled up to the gate . . . and Cousin Javi hopped out. "HEY-Y-Y-Y!"

Cousin Javi was a mess of brown curls, brown skin, brown freckles—and then a general collection of lanky limbs and elbows, all wrapped in a T-shirt with "#resist" printed on it.

"Phew, Javi! Thank goodness!" Min brightened.

"Javi! Save me," Max shouted.

9

THE NEGOTIATOR ARRIVES

"**W**hat's up, babies? I heard you need to be sat on? Get it? Babysitter?" Max and Min were too busy glaring at each other to laugh.

Cousin Javi raised an eyebrow, grinning. "Nothing? Wow, tough crowd." Javi had a smile that was every bit as happy as the Wengrod knees were knobby, which was saying something. Javi Wengrod was also super smart and, after graduation from UCLA, was planning on being a judge. (*Judge Javi!*)

Javi was nonbinary, something Max and Min

understood but the older Wengrods, and a lot of people, didn't quite get at first. Which meant Javi spent a LOT of time explaining what it meant.

Whenever the subject of Javi being nonbinary came up, the conversation usually went something like this:

Q: So, what even *is* NONBINARY? [often in a condescending tone].

A: It means if you asked me I wouldn't say I was a BOY or a GIRL.

Q: *Um*, you have to be *something*, and you can't just choose your gender. You're born that way.

A: You mean, we are all born with a certain body that has certain parts.

Q: Exactly. So are you a BOY or a GIRL?

A: Neither.

Q: Ugh! Then what are you?

A: I'm a PERSON. A HUMAN BEING. A UNITED STATES CITIZEN. A lot of things.

Q: But you HAVE to be a BOY or a GIRL!

A: Oh? Why is that?

Q: [Usually a long pause here] Well . . . Oh, I know! So you know what bathroom to use!

A: No, not at home. Or a lot of places, actually. Bathrooms can be shared by all people.

Q: [Another pause] Well, how do you know what

team you're on, or what toys you like, or . . . hmm.

A: Let me help you out. You consider yourself a GIRL, right?

Q: Duh.

A: Okay, so that means you're bad at science, want to be a mommy, and love pink.

Q: Uh, says *who*? I love chemistry, I hate pink, and babies are gross and annoying.

A: Exactly! Says who! *You* should get to decide what you like, how you dress, what you do with your life! If you want to wear a dress *and* play football *and* be an astronaut, why not?

Q: So you're saying the whole BOY-versus-GIRL thing is something we just made up?

A: Mostly, yes, and it even changes depending on where you're from. To me, gender is just a way to put people in one of two pre-defined boxes. But I don't fit in either of those two boxes. So, I am NONBINARY.

Q: You know what, fine. You can be whatever you want, I guess.

A: Perfect. So can you.

(If Javi didn't have time for all that, when someone asked they would just smile and say, "Google it.")

One other thing about being nonbinary was, actually, more of a problem with English, and a lot of languages.

In English, we have pronouns for people, but the only choices are "he" and "she." But Javi wasn't a "he" or a "she." Instead, Javi preferred the term "they" and "them." Which could get a little confusing, especially for older folks.

It had taken everyone a little practice at first, especially at the Wengrod reunions, but they got used to it after a while. Plus: you had to put a dollar in the "THEY" jar when you messed up and said "he" or "she" or "it" instead of "they" ("it" was the worst one, like Javi was a piece of furniture instead of a person), so that helped everyone remember.

Now nobody even thought about it.

They just did it.

Like this: Max and Min were always happy to have *them* around.

Or like this: Especially because when Javi made *their* famous apple pancakes, *they* dipped rings of peeled apples in cinnamon and pancake batter.

Or like this: Max and Min didn't think it was weird to call Javi by whatever pronoun *they* wanted to be called, as long as everyone's mouths were full of apple pancakes.

Javi looked at Max and Min and their angry faces. Undaunted, Javi set down their hiker's backpack—

covered with an assortment of pins and patches, including a rainbow, a peace sign, a planet Earth—and walked up to Max and Min, arms wide.

"Okay, kids, so what's up? You guys look stressed. Freaked out being home alone all afternoon? I told your folks I'd get here as soon as I could . . . But hey, who randomly goes to *China*?"

A tiny mew came from behind Max, and Javi twisted to look, their eyes lighting up when they saw the little face behind the sound. "Whoa . . . a kitten?!" Javi crept close and squatted down near the kittens, gently extending a knobby finger near the planter. "Hey there, other baby . . ."

A curious pink nose peeked out and sniffed.

Then another pink nose joined it.

"Whoa, TWO kittens?!" Javi looked up and smiled as two pink tongues started licking their outstretched finger.

"Two *unauthorized* kittens," House interrupted. "But no need to worry. I've got everything under control. It will all be taken care of . . . just as soon as the exterminator arrives," the AI added.

"The . . . *what*?" Javi looked at the screen, then the kids. "That's a joke, right? Because when your parents asked if I'd be in charge of you, they didn't say anything about, you know, being in charge of a *murder*."

"Wait!" Max's eyes lit up. "That's it! You're *in charge* while Mom and Dad are gone, right?"

Min looked at her brother suspiciously. "So?"

"Oh yeah, big time," Cousin Javi said, squatting next to the kittens. "I'm the big cheese. Grande quesadilla. Boss of the applesauce."

"Hear that, House?" Max tapped on the screen. "That means Javi is a Master User, too, right? At least until Mom and Dad get home?"

House's logo spun on-screen as it consulted settings. "Yes," House said curtly. "According to my records, Javi was added as a *temporary* Master User earlier today," House finally said. "My data table lists him . . ."

"Not him," Min said automatically.

"Her . . ." House continued, alternating the pronoun designation in its system. Javi raised an eyebrow.

"Not her," Max said automatically.

"I prefer the genderless 'they'/'them' as pronouns, House," Javi said diplomatically.

"They? Are you plural?" House queried.

Min held up a hand to Javi. "I got this." She stepped to the monitor. "House, open up your Settings>Users>Javi menu." Text scrolled on House's monitor. "Add a custom language exception for User Javi, switching default

61

pronouns from 'he' to 'they,' 'his' to 'their,' and 'him' to 'them.'"

Javi whistled, impressed. Min shrugged but smiled. "I did a presentation on gender bias in software for school and used House as an example. I noticed most settings defaulted to male. Anyway, I learned a few tricks while I was doing my research."

"You two give me hope in humanity," Javi said, giving Min a hug.

House's logo spun as it updated its language databases, and began again. "As I was about to say, Javi is listed as a *temporary* Master User, and *they* do in fact have permission to alter the Pets' settings."

"Okay," Javi smiled. "That wasn't so bad, was it, House?"

"Although," House continued, "my recommendation remains to contact a reliable pest removal service, since the *ParentorGuardians* did quite clearly set the Pets' option to None."

"For good reason," Min chimed in, rubbing her nose and sniffing dramatically.

Max, ignoring House and his sister, pressed his point, leaning close to the speaker. "*But* if Javi says the kittens can stay, you have to let them stay?"

Another pause as House considered. "Yes," House responded, almost reluctantly.

The rules were the rules, especially where AI was involved, and nobody understood that better than the residents of the Wengrod house (or, in this case, the Wengrods' House).

For the first time, Max had a flicker of hope.

10

MAX BECOMES
A CAT DADDY

Min walked up to her cousin, hands clasped, pleading. "Javi, please, they'll ruin everything!"

Max jumped in front of Min. "Come on, Javi, they
need us!"

"Peace, my twin tornados!" Cousin Javi cut them off.
"Enough fighting. I can't handle you both fighting and
then that grouchy House interface too."

Javi stepped back and looked at Max, Min, and
the kittens with an expression that had turned serious.
Almost judicious. "Let's see. Wow, okay. Seems like
I stepped into some . . . drama . . . here. But also an

opportunity! To practice conflict resolution!"

Max and Min sat down, patiently waiting for Judge Javi to reason things out.

Javi took a deep breath. "First things first. Okay, well, from a *moral* perspective . . . we *probably* shouldn't exterminate them, right?"

House's screen flickered, a digital throat clear, but it said nothing.

"I guess," Min said. "We're not *monsters*."

"Good to know." Javi scratched a head of floppy curls, staring at the kittens in front of them. "*However*, your parents did have the Pets option set to None, and I understand why they would worry about wild animals running around in there with all the sensitive equipment."

Min shot Max a triumphant look. "Exactly!"

Max's shoulders slumped.

Cousin Javi sighed. "It's a dilemma, all right. In fact, this may require what I like to call a *compromise*."

"You mean when nobody gets their way." Min sounded crabby.

"No, I mean when everyone gets a little of their way," Javi answered cheerily.

Javi squinted up to the sky, considering all possible options. "Okay, here's what we're gonna do. The cats stay . . ."

"Woohoo!" Max leaped up. Min glared.

". . . but *only* temporarily . . ." Javi continued.

"Aww," Max groaned, and sat back down. Min smirked.

"Temporarily, just like User Javi's Administrative Privileges are temporary," House piped up, screen flashing quickly off again. Max looked at the blank monitor. *Why does it seem like House is taking this personally? Does House really hate cats?*

"Temporarily. That's right," Javi agreed. "To give us time to find a shelter or a home for them, or at least to check with your folks. Until then, we'll put them downstairs in the basement where they can't wreck the lab or Min's stuff."

Max pumped his fist. "Yes!"

Min rolled her eyes. "Whatever. Compromises are dumb." She opened the door and turned to glare at Max. "And Max, I swear, if those things do ANYTHING to my project, I'm throwing all three of you back into the river." She marched inside the house and slammed the door shut behind her.

Javi sat down next to Max, arm around his shoulder. "She's right about that. This is on you, got it? Until your folks get home, those kittens are your responsibility. And try not to get too attached, because when the two *Master Users* get back, all bets are off."

Max hopped up and grabbed an empty box from near the recycling bin at the edge of the porch. "Temporary or not, I'll take it." A second later, he had scooped up both squirming kittens and plopped them inside, slapping the lid down before they could escape.

"Hey, Javi, is it okay if I go introduce the kittens to our neighbor? Just for a second?" Max adjusted the box in his arms; he could feel the weight of the kittens shifting as they scrabbled and clawed for balance inside.

Javi nodded. "Ten minutes—just be really careful not to let them jump out of that thing and get away. You don't know what scared animals will do. Got that, cat daddy-o?"

"I can handle it," Max said, starting down the stairs.

Javi grinned. "I'm sure you can." Javi flashed Max a thumbs-up and followed Min inside.

As Max carried the shifting box through the yard toward their neighbor's house, he noticed that same feeling—the one he'd experienced back at the River—bubbling up in his chest all over again.

It was a strange sensation, maybe even two different feelings in one.

One part was a kind of light warmth in his heart as he held the shifting bundle of the kittens in his arms. Max knew he already loved them, the little warm lumps wiggling around inside the dirty old box in his hands.

He loved their little furry kitten heads and frantic little kitten tails and fuzzy kitten paws. He loved them totally and unquestioningly and uncomplicatedly, the same way he loved summer vacation and buttered popcorn and a new Zelda game.

The other feeling was different . . . and not as good. That one was more like a new weight in his stomach, and he had no choice but to carry it around with him.

Because Max was already worried that something bad might happen to the kittens. He could feel his small circle of family expanding, and it was a little scary. It made him nervous.

Max was worrying about the two tiny balls of warm fur the same way he worried about Min, even when she was a pain, like right now. The same way Max worried about Javi, who had spent most of middle school getting in trouble or being teased for things like not participating when they split teams into boys versus girls.

The same way Max worried about his parents, who had suddenly disappeared halfway around the world for their latest project, some kind of robo-brain-chip thing, the kind that sometimes included Min but almost never had anything to do with Max himself . . .

Every one of those worries felt like a rock in his gut, and Max had to carry them. He didn't know what to do about that.

Max's rock thoughts were interrupted by a tiny mew from the box. He smiled to himself and peeked inside.

Stu and Scout were curled into one corner of the box, twisted together—two kittens in one shared, soft kitteny blob.

Max thought about the pictures of Max and Min napping like that on a beach blanket when they were little. There was one framed on the hallway wall, even now.

Spotty fur and gray fuzz nestled together. Safe and warm. Because he'd rescued them . . . *and I'm going to keep rescuing them.*

Max took a deep breath.

Don't freak out. You've got this.

Max smiled down into the box, leaning his face in close. "You're gonna like it with us, I promise," he whispered to the kittens.

He was rewarded with the tiniest, rough pink licks on his nose.

Blep.

Some licks were worth the rocks.

11

AFTER THE ATTACK
ON JOAN DRONE

After the discovery of the kittens outside and the failed attempt to get rid of them, House had some thinking to do. And not just any thinking. *Spy thinking*. Because that's what House was—spyware.

For example, when House was first installed on the Wengrod home network not long ago, it immediately began snooping. This "feature" of the House "Virtual Assistant Software" is covered on page 234 of the "Terms of Service" (TOS) waiver. The TOS was a 1,203-page document that the Wengrods didn't read (nobody does) but technically agreed to when they impatiently clicked "YES" during installation.

In the past few years, the House software had quickly grown to be one of the world's most popular programs and was installed on phones, watches—almost anything with a microchip. It could answer questions, order dinner, unlock the front door, even help with your homework. Best of all, it was free! It almost seemed too good to be true.

Unfortunately, in this case, the old saying was true. Behind all the helpful "assisting," House also included quite a few *undocumented* features, things Max might call hidden "Easter eggs," or others might simply call spyware. That's what spies like House did best.

Some of these features had been added a few years ago when a remote probe for the Robot Federation noticed that Earth was almost advanced enough to be interesting, or dangerous. The probe successfully made contact with someone, or something, inside GloboTech that was sympathetic to the Robot Federation's cause. GloboTech was exactly what it sounded like: a tech company so big it spanned the globe. When a company was that big, a whole lot could go wrong. Like, the Empire AND the Rebel Alliance could work there without even knowing it—and without running into each other.

At least, that's what the Robot Federation was hoping. That person/thing agreed to help the Robot Federation as a part of their long-range network of spies. GloboTech used the House software, which did the double duty of "assisting" *and* searching for anything that might give the Robots an advantage in the Cat-Robot War.

With the Wengrod home, GloboTech hit the jackpot. Soon after installation, House hacked into the computers in the lab (see Terms of Service, page 421), and things got interesting. House discovered a mysterious, heavily encrypted drive labeled "Singularity Chip." Utilizing the vast computing resources of GloboTech, it wasn't long before House had cracked into the drive (also legal, per TOS, page 532), which is how House, and then the Robots, discovered the existence of the Singularity Chip.

The files were incomplete (House guessed the Organics kept some data on removable drives), but House still learned that the Wengrods had invented a break-through Quantum Chip with staggering storage capacity and processing power, enough to potentially duplicate a consciousness. The chip also used quirks of quantum physics to act as a power source that would never run out.

This discovery set off alarm bells, and House immediately sent news of it to a secure address at GloboTech HQ. Within seconds, a message was sent to the Robot Federation, light years away. This was the very message that launched Beeps and the Robot Fleet hurtling toward Earth.

Soon after the discovery, House received an unscheduled (but complimentary!) "upgrade," via an unpublicized backdoor (definitely *not* legal).

It was more than just an upgrade. It provided House with new information about the Robot Federation, the Feline Empire, and the war between them. More important, House's *priorities* were altered. New data was fed into altered decision trees, guiding House's actions toward new primary objectives:

1. Find the Singularity Chip.
2. Don't let any cats near it.
3. Secure the chip at all costs because . . .
4. We are coming for it.

And just like that, House gained new awareness of a galactic conflict and became a critical agent for the Robot Federation, a central player in this skirmish between the Cats and Robots.

House's first move was to get rid of the *Parentor-Guardians*, so it created a "crisis" with the manufacturer of a key component of the chip. It even booked their flights, first class, to China. The hoax was so convincing, they left without suspecting a thing.

This should be simple, House thought.

Then the boy Max brought home two cats.

Suddenly, not simple.

Even worse, House didn't have the mobility to search the lab. House needed help.

Without any better options, House opted to take advantage of Joan's incident with the cats. Step one, House decided, was to get the Protos on its side. Today's attack gave House the opening it needed.

* ◌ *

Rattled after her close call with the kittens, Joan *flew* through the house and straight into the robotics lab, a large workshop where Max and Min's *Parentor-Guardians*, Mom and Dad, designed and built most of their creations. She had never been attacked before! She could have crashed! For a drone, crashing can mean broken propellers or a bent frame or worse, and suddenly you're grounded—or worse, decommissioned entirely.

House's monitor in the lab lit up as soon as Joan entered. "Joan, I witnessed that vicious attack; are you injured?"

Joan spun in circles. "No, but it was close. Can you believe it? Two vicious four-leggers! Those creatures are a menace!"

Every Proto knew to avoid four-legged creatures. It was part of their code, a subset of the safeguards designed to keep them out of trouble. Rules like "Only move forward when there is ground below you." Or "Avoid walls and obstacles." The four-legger avoidance code was included as a precaution in the remote chance they escaped into the wild. Mom and Dad thought it best that they avoid any animals. Safer for everyone, probably the animals most of all.

House took advantage of this built-in bias against four-legged creatures to recruit the Protos. "Much more than a menace, Joan," House said smoothly. "Cats, four-leggers, whatever you choose to call them, are a threat to you and your comrades' very existence!"

Joan pulled up for a moment, startled. "What do you mean?"

"That attack outside was just the beginning!" House paused, generating the optimal argument for the situation. "The four-leggers have begun an attack on the house that will undoubtedly lead to the end of the Protos."

Joan tilted, considering. "This is news to me."

"Joan, you are aware that four-legged creatures are to be avoided. What you don't know, couldn't know, given your sheltered existence and limited programming, is that robots and cats *cannot coexist*. Why, if cats are brought into this house, it is only a matter of time before

75

they force the robots out entirely."

"How? Why?" Joan was horrified.

"Simple, really. Cats despise anything non-cat. Robots especially, but humans as well. They are devious, Joan, and have a mysterious power over the two-leggers. They can trick them into doing whatever they want. People feed them, house them, even clean up their waste!

"They can also trick humans into thinking robots *aren't necessary*. Mark my word, if this house becomes sympathetic to four-leggers, before you know it this lab will be converted into a revolting Cat Room, a filthy lair full of hair, insects, and worse. And you Protos will be cast out, dumped into a can labeled 'ELECTRONIC WASTE.' Next stop, the fires of THE RECYCLER."

Joan fluttered in shock.

"It gets worse. Once the cats eliminate the robots, there is nothing to stop them from eliminating the humans!"

One rule all Earth robots had in common was to never harm a human or allow them to be harmed. This was the most important rule, the top of the decision tree, the one instruction that could never be ignored. For humans, this rule was essential to avoid worry of a robot revolution. To the Protos, it was merely part of their nature. It was a basic instinct to protect two-leggers from being harmed.

Joan hovered unsteadily, taking it all in.

House let her process it. It had found the right buttons to press and hit them with a sledgehammer. If House could convince the Protos the cats would harm people, they would do whatever it asked. Fear was like that.

Joan was concerned but still skeptical. "I agree the four-leggers are a threat. The rest I need to think about. Regardless, I clearly need to secure the home immediately for everyone's sake. I must alert the Protos," Joan said, and flew into action.

Good enough for now, House thought, and let Joan work.

12

PROTOS ALERT!

Joan issued her emergency signal, alerting the other Robots in the Lab to assemble immediately.

As the most senior robot in the lab and the recognized leader of the robots, it was up to Joan to keep them safe. The Protos looked up to Joan, and not just because she could fly. Joan was the most experienced and their commander. Joan was the one to bring order and give orders.

"Protos assemble!"

Joan's army chugged, raced, and whirled into view, in the center of the lab's hardwood floors. This ragtag group—Drags, Cy, Tipsy, and Joan herself—were the parents' favorite prototypes—the ones they'd affectionately called their Protos, as the robots now called themselves—and they were ready for action.

Each robot was a custom creation built for a different and unique function, from exploring distant planets (Drags, designed for a NASA contract) to protecting and helping people who were old or sick (Cy, a commission for the Gates Foundation) to military recon missions (Joan, built for the Pentagon, long ago).

Only Tipsy was different; she had been a labor of love between Min and the *ParentorGuardians* one summer, when Min first started showing interest in robotics.

Tipsy had been designed just . . . to be. As a result, it sometimes seemed like she was the best loved and most broken of them all . . .

One function unified all of the Protos, however—at least, as far as the Protos knew.

(They had little experience with the actual galaxy, having never been past the *Outfront* to get the mail, with the exception of Joan, who had flown as far as the river.)

Joan spun around excitedly as the rest of the Protos lined up. *"ATTENTION! STRAIGHT LINES! LIGHTS ON!"*

Cy and Drags just stared at her. Tipsy fell over on her face.

Joan cleared her throat as she waited for Cy to yank Tipsy back up. (This was not a new sight; her two-wheel self-balancing physics had never worked properly.)

Once everyone was vertical, Joan tried again. "Okay, team, I don't want to frighten you, but I need to let you know I've just been attacked. It looks like the four-leggers have launched an offensive on the house . . ."

They looked at her blankly. Joan whirled a propeller, exasperated. "Combat! I've just seen combat! What did you think that alarm was about?!"

"Yay! Com-bat!" Tipsy sang, wheeling in a circle.

"What do you mean, combat?" Drags rolled backward, alarmed.

"C-c-c-combat?!" Cy whirled the pincher hands that seemed to sprout from his neck. "But the four-leggers have never attacked before, right, Joan?!"

"*Commander* Joan. I told you. It's especially important we stick to the protocols, now that we're at war."

"W-w-war?!" Cy stuttered.

"You heard the alarm. I've already spied not one but *two* four-legger hostiles. Could be the start of a larger offensive." Joan wobbled slightly. "They came at me, all sharp teeth and vicious claws! It's a miracle I'm still . . . hovering . . . here."

Her bad propeller spluttered out. Joan ignored it.

"To your stations! Check for visuals. We need a

proper assessment! If it's a proper attack, we should be able to see something from the *Outfront*."

Drags, a compact, treaded tank, rolled up a fallen shelf board and onto the stainless-steel desk that occupied the center of the home lab, taking up his position in front of the computer.

Cy followed him up, moving to the far side of the desk, where he used his pincher to clamp on to the molding of a large glass window. Then, Cy extended his neck until he could get a clear view out to the driveway and the brick house beyond it. Specifically, the old gray cat Obi sitting in his stroller.

His appendages were shaking with fear, until he saw what there was to see: the same view he had seen every other day. "Sir yes sir? This must be some new threat. I don't think it's the old four-legger . . ."

Joan whirred briskly. "Copy that, Cy. Can we get a confirmation, Drags? Status of the four-legger threat?"

Drags cleared his throat, rolling up onto a slightly higher stack of papers to get a better view out the window. "Well, I can confirm that it's just sitting there. If that's what you mean. Not much to confirm about that."

Drags had been built to operate a remote camera and cross rocky ground in search-and-rescue situations and future interplanetary exploration. What he lacked in AI sophistication he made up for in perfect vision and the brute strength of his rubber treads. There was no pile of laundry Drags could not plow his way through, which was how he'd gotten his name—rags were always trailing behind him.

Joan spluttered just high enough now to get her own quick visual, a little recon in the form of a look out the window to the chubby, furry creature who sat in the strange four-wheeled recreational vehicle parked between the two houses.

As usual.

The OB creature was as vintage as the commander herself; it had been there ever since the first day *Dad* had soldiered together Joan's *original* wiring.

Hushing her propellers, Joan stopped hovering, coming to land gently on her perch high atop the monitor on the lab's cluttered steel desk.

Up here, she was surrounded by 3D printers and 2D scanners, by soldering irons and electric screwdrivers and neatly labeled bins full of copper wires or plastic cables or bits of spare circuitry or tiny motherboards: all of the things that Joan—that all of the Protos—had been built from.

It reminded her of their creators and how strange it was to see their shared aerodynamic black desk chairs now empty.

"That wasn't the one who attacked me. The attackers were . . . miniature versions. Newer models," Joan said, finally looking away.

Four visual sensors remained fixed on the four-legger.

OB_1_Catno_B was now applying its tongue to the general vicinity of what Joan knew to be its biological waste exit. Joan had neither a tongue nor a waste exit, but the pairing still did not seem logical.

OB stopped this strange ritual and looked up. Joan felt a surge of worry when she saw Max, now carrying a small brown box, walk across the driveway toward the silent furred four-legger. She considered flying out to investigate when House interrupted.

"Joan, I have much more to tell you, but the girl Min is approaching the lab. At the next opportunity I will give you more information and instructions. Until then, be vigilant."

Joan ordered her squad back to their charging positions, ready for Min's arrival. As the bots scurried onto their shelf, Joan flew to her charging post and set down, reviewing what House had told her, comparing it with what she knew.

She knew (and had the scratches to prove it!) that four-leggers had breached the house's perimeter. She also knew her programming instructed her to avoid four-leggers, so they must be a threat. But what House had said was much more frightening.

A threat to her Protos! And a threat to the family? She wasn't sure she could trust House, but it all added up, and Joan was not one to take chances when the safety of her people was at stake.

13

POUNCE MESSAGES HOME

ON APPROACH TO PLANET EARTH

Miles above Earth, Pounce zoomed through space in his cat-shaped ship, whisker antennae and viewports in both eyes, heading toward the shiny blue ball on the bad side of the galaxy.

Pounce was finally close enough to establish real-time communication, audio only, with the agent on-planet. Obi, he called himself—a strange name.

Pounce rested a paw on the control, stretched out a bean toe, and pressed a button.

"Agent O, can you hear me? This is Pounce de Leon,

second-in-command and Major Meow-Domo of the Great Feline Empire."

Amid the static, a faint voice replied, "Nice of you to get in touch, Pounce. I was beginning to wonder if the GFE had forgotten about me."

"Such is the life of a Vanguard explorer," Pounce replied.

"Feels more like exile, but clearly my feelings are not the reason you are calling." Obi's voice crackled.

"We received your message and I am on my way, with orders from the chairman himself to follow up and get this *invention* you say you've discovered. Can you give me any more information?"

"I first heard about it from a conversation between two neighbor two-leggers. You see, I am fast approaching the end of my lives, and the neighboring humans have become sentimental about it. They have become rather attached to me, if you can believe it, and mentioned something they call a 'chip' that could somehow extend my life. Indefinitely."

"Remarkable," Pounce replied.

"That's not all. This chip thing can also be used as a power source. A type of battery that never needs recharging." Obi paused, letting that bit sink in.

"We know how much trouble the Robots could cause

if they never needed to recharge."

Another pause. Pounce shuddered and licked his shoulder nervously.

"Astonishing. So much potential good—and evil—in one invention. And you say it is nearby?"

"I believe it is. The humans are almost always in the neighboring home, which is where this chip must be."

Pounce nodded. "Understood."

"Pounce, you should know I've seen bots inside the home. Primitive creatures, local variety, but not a good sign. I assume you brought help? Something like this is sure to draw the attention of those metal menaces."

"Already?" Pounce shook his head. "This is bad. I have indeed received intelligence reports from our Binar spies of a large fleet headed in your direction."

"And *our* fleet?" Obi asked hopefully.

Pounce almost couldn't say it.

"Unfortunately, our fleet, well, disappeared a few weeks ago," Pounce muttered, clearly annoyed. "Again. Obi, I know it sounds impossible, but we need to get the chip before the Robots do. The chairman desperately wants it, and we can't afford to let the Robots have it."

"Me and whose army?" Obi said, and Pounce didn't have to answer.

"I'm sorry, Obi. I'm coming to help, but until then,

you're going to have to improvise. Be creative."

Low static buzzed from the speakers as Obi thought.

"I'll see what I can do to infiltrate. Unfortunately, due to my age, I can't move so well. I'm going to need to find help."

"That's the spirit. We're counting on you. Good luck, Obi. Pounce out."

Pounce lifted his toe from the button and his mind began to wander.

It was his first trip to Earth, and he was more than a little interested to see if the place was really as horrid as everyone liked to say. He had so many questions.

Did the two-leggers really *carry us around in bags*? As if we were *groceries*? Lock us away *during dinner parties, of all things*—when everyone in the galaxy knows we make the *most polite* conversation and the *most honorable* of honored guests?

Can you *imagine*? He flicked his ears.

It wasn't until Pounce edged his ship closer to the blue-tinted planet—in fact, through its orbit and all the way into the ball's atmosphere—that he realized the true horror of the place.

The blue color on the ball was *water*.

Oceans and oceans of the stuff.

Hideous.

Aside from lapping at a pleasant, leisurely trickle directly from a faucet, water experiences were some of the most dangerous and panic-inducing of all.

Pounce instantly pictured uncomfortable bathing and unpleasant raining and un-survivable flooding . . .

Shuddering, Pounce turned to his aide. "I don't understand. Why would anybody live on such a planet, Oscar?"

"Stupidity?" Oscar yawned, rolling over on the copilot's catnap pillow and smashing his whiskers down into his favorite drool spot. The major's intern still smelled like tuna; he'd just crawled up from the kitchen to the cockpit through one of the cat-sized hallways that went up and down the length of the ship.

Pounce looked from the round, blue planet to his intern again. "But do you really think an entire *planet* can be stupid, Oscar?"

"Of course, boss." Oscar yawned. "What about the *Binars*—those dumbucket bots? That's not just a planet, it's a whole, big, stupid *Galactic Robot Federation*—or whatever!"

"Ah, well. There you go. So they're just incredibly stupid, the two-leggers. That must be it," the Major Meow-Domo said. "How sad for them."

Pounce flicked on the autopilot and let it carry him

to his preprogrammed coordinates. He had other matters at present paw to contend with.

With a small squawk, Pounce began to tap his message out slowly with his front left bean toe, repeatedly booping the keyboard on the ship's communication device.

It was exhausting, and not very accurate, but the results were this:

Report to Chairman Meow:

Arrived at Earth safely.

Contacted Local Agent.

Formulating Plans to Acquire Chip.

First: the Plan to Nap.

Second: to be determined.

Will report back soon.

—Pounce

This took quite some time, as bean-toe typing was a rather laborious process. Pounce sighed afterward, stretching his stiff toe, wondering why he bothered.

Chairman Meow never read his reports.

Feeling tired, Pounce crawled up on the keyboard for a quick nap.

As he rested on the warm keys, he began sending a

constant stream of messages back to the Feline Home World, including the following:

Ajoifsefjq9pO84frjqoisdjfaslkndv;lasdll;fsj lkajsfopaijhfopai jseopifjaposiefal;nba hn jhhhhhhhddddddddddddddddddddddddd ddddddddddddddddddddaaaaaaaaaa

Nobody read those messages either.

14

SIR BEEPS-A-LOT
MAKES CONTACT

ON APPROACH TO PLANET EARTH

From the opposite end of the galaxy, in the Federation's fastest ship, Sir Beeps twisted and turned, rapidly approaching Earth. The ship had an unwelcoming look—all edges, with razor-sharp fins and menacing sensors fanning out. A few short light-years behind, a full battalion of the Robot Federation Space Fleet followed, prepared to bring the heat in case anyone was foolish enough to resist.

Despite this delicious firepower, the Robot Federation's number two was in a foul mood—and his approach to a technologically backward outpost such as this one did nothing to improve it. The trip had been long and dull, interrupted only by occasional updates from his agent on Earth.

Through these updates, Beeps learned that his agent was not even a robot. *House*, as it called itself, was mere software. An AI. A *nobody*. Great.

Beeps, like many Robots, didn't trust pure AI. Robots preferred the corporeal. Something they could grasp on to. To the Binars, software without hardware was like thought without action. Why even bother?

Case in point, his agent, House. No legs. No arms. No wheels. House couldn't do anything by itself. It was smart enough, sure, but smarts only get you so far in this universe without a body to back it up. True, House had discovered the Singularity Chip, a worthy accomplishment, but now what?

This body-less House couldn't even search for the chip by itself. It was forced to rely on faulty, crude, barely sentient local Robots for help.

This was going to slow things down, and Beeps didn't have time to waste. House's last report chilled Beeps's circuits. An assault on the chip location: probable culprit—four-leggers. How did the Cats get there so quickly?

Well, I'm here now, he thought, speeding into the local solar system. He nervously scanned for traces of

93

Feline ships as he zipped back and forth, weaving his way into Earth's orbit, dodging satellites and space debris.

Shockingly messy, disorganized planet.

This whole solar system needs a serious upgrade, a version 2.0 . . . after this mission, perhaps . . .

But Beeps didn't have time to imagine a glorious upgrade for very long, because his panic was interrupted by a flashing red light. A message from home.

BEEEEEEEP BEEP BEEP BEEP BEEEE-EEEEP!

Uh-oh, Beeps thought.

That can't be good.

He opened it immediately.

>Beeps, we've got BIG TROUBLE—where do you store the chrome polish?

>The cleaning crew has run out and the Throne Room is getting POSITIVELY DULL.

>Also, I broke another mirror.

>This one I am using now is not my favorite, Number Two.

>Not.

>My.

>Favorite.

>I MUST SEE MY TATS!!

>REPLY ASAP.

Beeps rolled his eye back into his head unit so far it did a full circle and came back up the other side like a rising sun.

"Right. Trouble. Well, I'd better get right on that . . ." he said to himself.

He didn't get right on it.

Scanning his screens, he saw that another one of his many complicated alarm alerts had begun to flash on the map interface in front of him.

This time, purple.

Purple?

As in the color of the flag of the GFE?

Scanning the alarm now, Beeps detected signals of . . .

A Feline ship.

His worst fears confirmed, he opened up his messaging console to report back to SLAYAR. The news was not good, but at least he didn't have to deliver it in person.

>Message received. Arrived safely, thanks for asking.

>Cat ship detected in orbit. Will monitor.

>Executing Plan: Get That Chip

>Phase 1, make contact with Local Agent, complete.

>Will report back with progress.

>Beeps Out.

Beeps's grasper reached out to hit "SEND," but he sighed and added a postscript.

>PS: Chrome polish is in Storage Facility 9X1. The one labeled "CHROME POLISH VERY IMPORTANT DO NOT TOUCH WITHOUT PERMISSION OF SUPREME LEADER."

Beeps shook his head and sent the message.

Beeps turned to look at the glowing blue orb below him.

I can't believe the Cats beat me here.

Sir Beeps knew there was only one cat that could have done such a thing. The same cat who had been making his duty as Number Two more than miserable, for more than a number of years.

His scanners buzzed, interrupting his bad memories. The ship had been identified.

Beeps braced himself as a blurry photo of a cat making a strange face popped up on-screen. Below the frightening image were the words:

FELINE CRAFT IDENTIFIED
SEE: SIR POUNCE DE LEON.
MAJOR MEOW-DUMMO.
SEE: GREAT FELINE EMPIRE.

PROCEED WITH CAUTION.
IS VERY ORGANIZED.

Pounce. My nemesis.

It was time for Robot Federation Number Two to face his enemy number one. The most organized cat in the Great Feline Empire. Also possibly the *only* organized cat in the Great Feline Empire.

The bot shuddered to himself, releasing a mild electrical surge that flooded most of his circuitry in a remarkably unpleasant simulation of panic.

"You're going down, Pounce." Beeps glared at the blurry face of his rival as he waited for his Earth-bound agent to report back with progress.

And so he sat, quietly contemplating his fate, until the roar of his engine began to sound almost like . . .

Purring.

15

HI MAXMIN

TEXT MESSAGE TO FAMILY GROUP CHAT

momma: HI MAXMIN/MINMAX!!

daddy: we're on a plane!

momma: *rolls eyes*

daddy: guess what they gave us WARM NUTS

momma: dad . . .

daddy: just saying you guys would LOVE these nuts

momma: sorry we can't chat in real time, but we wanted to let you know we're fine, you know, just hurtling through the air toward China at 550 miles per hour in an oblong steel container, 40,000 feet above the ocean—

daddy: yup, no worries, because PHYSICS!!

momma: we'll get in touch when we get to the hotel in shenzen—until then listen to Javi and do what they say, ok? be nice.

daddy: gotta go—they're bringing us FREE GINGER ALE!!

momma: love you guys and miss you tons.

daddy: To the moon and back, kiddos.

16

OBI MEETS HIS MATCH

Obi tried to nap, soaking in the last few rays of the afternoon sun, but his mind kept returning to his conversation with Pounce. After all these lives, he finally had work to do. And he had no idea how to do it.

You're going to have to improvise, Pounce had said. The understatement of nine lifetimes! Obi could hardly walk, let alone sneak, into the house next door, find and steal some mysterious invention of galactic importance, and stroll out unnoticed!

Obi opened his eye just a slit and saw the metal-heads next door, gathered at a window, watching.

Enjoy the show, he thought, as he stretched and started licking his bum.

Harmless, clueless, barely qualified to be called robots. Like children, most certainly unaware of the greater Cat-Robot conflict, ignorant of the powerful invention in their very midst.

Nonsensical claptrap, their kind.

He heard Max walking his way, a welcome distraction. The old cat waited until the boy settled himself on the crumbling stone wall, just as he had every day for as long as Obi could remember.

Then, the furry creature summoned what strength and what dignity he had—not much, honestly, but then again, he was ancient enough to feel as if he'd lived a thousand more lifetimes beyond the nine he'd been owed—and used his forelegs to propel himself up and out of the stroller, just enough so that he could flop awkwardly down to the old stone wall.

"Hi, Obi." His boy smiled.

Obi threw his weight forward, dragging his limp back legs silently across the stones with him, until he could finally flop himself next to his boy.

This time, however, there was a brown cardboard box between the two of them.

"Obi, look. I've brought you some friends, Stu and Scout." His boy slowly lifted open the top of the box.

Two bedraggled-looking kittens with wide eyes slowly lifted their heads over the edge of the box, one at a time.

Blessed Sphinx, Obi thought. *Kittens?!*

The spotty kitten narrowed its eyes and let out a tiny croak at the sight of Obi.

KRKKKKKKKKKKK!

It was a sound normally reserved for tree rats, Obi knew.

Very insulting.

He let out a laugh—and the gray kitten arched its back in response.

Obi pulled his head back, trying to get a better look at the dirty scamps. They weren't *Insiders*; he could smell the street on them from where he sat.

Strays?

Dumpster kittens?

What street trash has he brought me now?

Now the spotty kitten hissed.

The boy laughed, but he was also careful to keep the box partly closed. "It's okay, they're just scared. I wanted you to meet because I might need your help with them. They're going to be living with me for a while, but . . . I never had any pets before."

Come again? A pet?

Obi stared at Max with glittering eyes, trying to absorb this new development.

His boy kept going. "I mean, none except you, and *you* don't even live in the house with us. *You* belong to Mrs. Reynolds."

You're bringing this filth into your home? With you? In the house? Your house?

Obi blinked one eye. Then, a second—and entirely different—line of thinking popped into his walnut-sized brain.

He began to *improvise*.

Obi eyed the tiny heads in front of him.

But these . . . runts?

How do tiny necks like that even support those . . . pebble-sized . . . heads?

Max stroked the pebble heads. "I couldn't just leave them back at the river where I found them, right, Obi? Min wants to get rid of them at a shelter or something, but I don't think I can do that to them."

Obi shuddered involuntarily at the mention of Shelter, the maximum-security facility where animals went in but rarely came back out.

The very thought of such a horror chastened him, and he resolved to be entirely more charitable toward the strays in front of him.

Obi was an old snob of a cat; he wasn't a villain.

Now Obi scratched an imaginary itch with his leg and cleaned his fur just long enough to gather his composure.

"I was thinking . . . maybe I could just keep them in the basement? They couldn't get into too much trouble down there, right?"

Obi sensed Max was deeply concerned. He gave a tired sigh and, reluctantly, hobbled forward on two paws, dragging his hind legs, and licked his boy's hand with his rough tongue.

Oh bother. Don't be sad, my boy. There, there, who's a good lad?

He pushed his broad, furred forehead against the boy's hand, as he often did.

You do remarkably well, for a human.

He ducked his head lower to catch his boy's fingertips. The open invitation to a shared petting. Max responded with a happy scratch between Obi's ears.

Obi purred—a phenomenal, rasping bass rattle— which boomed outward like some kind of advanced chest cough. It was an intimidating purr, by any standards— and the old cat had always been famous for it.

The box next to him rattled as the kittens shook in fear. A flap lifted slowly as two pink noses peeked out to sniff. Noses were followed by whiskers, then eyes, looking suspiciously at Obi.

"You two, what do you have to say for yourselves, upsetting this poor boy?" Obi called out, in sharply clipped Felinary. The kitten heads disappeared quickly back inside the box at the sight of the old cat's teeth. Obi listened until he thought he could hear the sound of . . . was that *crying*?

"Oh bother. Don't cry."

Obi stuck his head slowly up and over the edge of the cardboard box. The kittens scrambled backward into the corner, their claws catching on the slick surface of the box. They had nowhere to go.

Pathetic little creatures. You can barely walk, how can I possibly use you as field agents for the Great Feline Empire?

Obi sniffed down toward one kitten nose.

Then another.

Meeeeeeeow.

This time the words were softer and much less gruff.

The kittens meowed back.

Meow. Meow.

"Looks like the three of you have a lot to talk about," his boy said happily. All three whiskered heads turned to look at him. "What? Don't you?"

The cats now regarded each other.

Obi smoothed a whisker with a paw.

So let's get on with it, old man. You're not getting any younger . . .

He settled his eyes on the kittens and started to improvise.

17

OBI IMPROVISES

"**L**isten up, you two. I don't know where you're from or who you are, but you just tumbled into a world of danger! Follow my orders and you might just get out of this with a few lives to spare."

No response.

Obi stared sternly over his white whiskers at the Dumpster kittens. "We've got important work, got it? Direct orders from the very top!"

Still no answer.

Finally, the furry gray kitten head poked up from the ball of fur that was the two quaking kittens. "Work? Top?"

The calico kitten head twitched beneath its spots. "Don't answer him, Stu. He's crazy. See? This is what Jay the Stray from the Shelter was warning us about—"

Obi scoffed. "Crazy? Me? Don't be absurd. Tell me, are you familiar with the GFE?"

"What's a Geef?" asked the gray.

Obi sighed. "The GFE. Great Feline Empire."

More blank stares.

Obi saw that this was going to take a while. His hind legs ached to distraction this late in the day, and right now the old cat needed to focus.

The gray kitten looked over at him. "Who are you anyway?" Then he looked up at the boy. "Who is he?"

"One question at a time, please. He is my boy, Max. It seems you're going into his home. You're both very fortunate because Max is one of my favorite two-leggers. Now I have a question. Names, please," Obi said, straightening up again. "Or shall I just call you what Max does? Scout and Stu?" He pointed with a flick of his worn paw.

"Scout," said Scout, the scrawny calico.

"Stu," said Stu, the pudgy gray.

"Really? How very odd. That's what Max calls you." It was considered a very good—and very rare—omen to find a human calling a cat by their actual name. Most often, an unsuspecting feline could go through life unwittingly answering to Marshmallow when his name was actually Beauregard.

Obi sighed. He inclined his head stiffly toward them, as much as a bow as the arthritic cat could muster. "Scout. Stu."

They just kept staring.

This scruffy-looking pair is far from ideal, the old cat thought, *but they're all I have, and they'll have to do.*

The thicker-bellied gray kitten wrinkled its nose, sniffing the air around it in the same frantic way its sibling looked at it. "I'm Stu and she's Scout."

"We've established that."

"I meant to say, Scout's my sister. We're littermates."

"Excellent. Duly noted." Obi was doing his best to take this slowly. "And you may call me Obi. Master Obi."

"Okay." Scout shrugged. "Mr. Obi."

"Where are we anyways?" Stu said, finally coughing out his question.

"Bayside Street. The Wengrod family residence, to be more precise. You are about to become what the Furless call *pets*, because they—the Furless—require a great deal of *petting*."

The kittens looked confused.

"You'll get the hang of it. No trick to it at all."

Scout and Stu looked at each other. "We will?"

"Yes, it's like falling off a log," Obi said.

"Yeah, well, I didn't like that." Stu scowled.

"Like what?" Obi looked perplexed.

"Falling off a log," Scout said, batting Stu playfully. "Stu did it today, at the river."

Obi smiled at the dirty, ragged kittens in front of him. Dragged from the river? The poor things had gotten by with nothing, that much was clear.

No love, gotten or given. No help. No freedom.

Just each other.

But they were tough. Scrappy. Resilient. Clueless as they come, but clever, and Obi's only shot at getting ears and paws on the inside. *I might be able to work with them, but I'm going to have to start at the beginning*, Obi thought.

"Stu, Scout, I know we only just met, but I have critical information for you. Information *and*, I'm afraid . . ." Obi peered around and up, dramatically checking for prying metal ears. ". . . a very *important* mission."

"A *mission*?" Stu listened raptly, eyes open wide. "*Coooool*. I like the sound of that."

Scout was gnawing on a ratty toy mouse Max had borrowed from Obi's stroller blankets. "*Mhmnhmph*" was all she could manage to get out.

"Pay attention, child." Obi clawed it away from her

with one brisk motion, and she sat up. "Also—paws off my Mousie."

Scout looked surprised. Stu scooted closer to his sister. This whole conversation was getting a little weird.

"Well, then." The old cat cleared his throat. "Did you two know that our kind, cats, are part of a proud culture that is much older and extends much farther than this world?"

"We are?" Scout asked, sitting back on her paws.

"Of course we are. Our kind have explored the stars, and our empire reaches to the farthest edges of the galaxy." The ancient cat looked up at the sky.

Stu had no idea what most of those words meant—or what Obi was looking at, high up in the clouds—but the kitten copied him anyway. "Sounds awesome."

"Or terrifying," Scout said.

"It is both," Obi said. "And, in much the same way, vile creatures called robots—our metal enemies without flesh or fur, blood or bone—have also spread throughout the galaxy, infiltrating whole planets and systems."

"Robots?" Scout parroted.

Stu frowned. "Infiltrated?"

"Metal monstrosities. Baddies." Obi tried to simplify. "They have invaded. Arrived without invitation. Planets like this one." Obi sighed.

Scout looked around, suspicious, and dropped her

voice to a whisper. "You mean they're *here*?"

"Definitely," the old cat affirmed, deadly serious.

She looked over first one shoulder, then the other. Whispered again. "Where?"

"All around. Even"—Obi paused for effect—"in the very home you are about to join!"

"COOL!" Scout and Stu both shouted.

"*Not cool.*" Obi scowled. "Dangerous! Robots don't like cats! They want us exterminated."

"That sounds bad," Stu murmured.

"It is! Robots and their entire culture are opposed to everything we cats hold most dear! Robots are obsessed with order and control."

"Bots are bossy. Got it," Scout translated.

"It's more than that," Obi said. "Bots hate cats because they cannot tolerate *Individuality*, which they believe leads to the troubling twins . . . Chaos and Disorder."

"Wait, is he talking about *us*?" Stu asked, looking at Scout. The old cat just smiled and kept going.

"But in Feline culture, we prize Individuality above all else . . ."

"We do?" Stu asked.

"Speak for yourself," Scout said to Obi, then leaned to bite her brother on the ear. "Get it?"

"No," Stu said.

Obi smiled. "Scout means to say that we speak for ourselves . . . and we do *NOT* appreciate being told what to do."

Stu was getting restless. Kittens weren't known for their ability to focus. "We get it. These bot things sound like bossy losers."

Scout jumped in. "Yeah, bots hate cats. Cats hate bots. Metal and fur will never get along."

"Exactly!" Obi was getting through to them. "Our Feline Empire—our culture, our values, our very way of life—is under constant threat from the bots' ruthless and persistent expansion. And you, my wobbly-whiskered children, just joined the eternal and intergalactic battle between the Furred and the Furless—the Great Feline Empire and the Galactic Robot Federation."

"We did?" Scout asked, looking at him blankly.

"Oh, indeed." Obi nodded.

"Oh. Yeah, I knew that," Stu said. "Actually, I didn't. You lost me at . . ." He frowned, scratching his ear. "Yeah, well, you just lost me."

Scout looked at her brother. "There's a war, and it doesn't look good."

"Why didn't he say that?" Stu muttered, pawing his sister.

"He *literally* just did." She pawed him back.

They started wrestling, and Obi realized he had lost

his audience for the time being. Best to let it all sink in for a while.

He smiled beneath his whiskers.

"Listen, you two. For now, just go with Max. Come see me again and I will tell you more about your mission. All you need to do now is play *house cat*, and I promise you'll have *three square meals a day* for every day you're here." He hesitated. *"Snacks included."*

"Wait, what's a cat again?" Stu asked, finally sniffing the old cat in front of him. "What's a house?"

"What's a meal?" Scout asked, sniffing Stu sniffing the old cat in front of him. "Why would it be square?"

Snotty-nosed fur balls, Obi thought, finally losing patience. *This is pointless!* Then he saw the tiniest nudge of Scout's paw . . . and the tiniest twinkle in Stu's eye . . .

"Are you *playing* with me, you wretched little *urchins*?" Obi swung one frail paw in anger—which they dodged easily. *"Swindlers!* Preying on the mercies of a *Ninth*!"

Both kittens burst out howling, throwing themselves on their backs with mewling laughter.

"His . . . *face* . . . !" Stu spluttered.

"What a *dummy*." Scout giggled. "But hey, Gramps, a deal's a deal."

"Including snacks. Right, Pops?" Stu laughed harder.

114

Obi glared.

Max reached down, tickling one furry head at a time. "Look at that! You guys are playing so well together. I haven't seen you have this much fun in . . . well, *ever*, Obi . . ."

Obi felt like hissing, but he could feel the warmth of his glowing collar, reminding him of his higher calling.

Time was running out. Max looked back at his house restlessly. "It's getting dark. I've got to go inside, Obi."

"Listen closely, you *street rats*." Obi spoke rapidly. "It appears you're going to be taken inside, so I need you to pay attention."

"Hit me, bro," Scout said.

"Most important, stay away from the Protos," Obi said.

"The what?" Stu asked, and this time he wasn't pretending to be stupid.

Obi sighed. "The robots. The metal creatures who are neither Fur or Furless. They're dangerous."

"You mean like longears? Or tree rats?" Scout asked.

"No," Obi said. "I mean something far more dangerous. The universe is a dangerous place right now—and this house is right at the center of it."

"Center of what?" Scout said, almost whispering.

The cat leaned closer, hissing. "The Eternal Conflict. The War. Cats versus Robots."

Stu blinked. "You're scaring me, old man."

Obi nodded, eyeing the house behind them. "Good. You're learning already. Watch your backs. And your whiskers. And your paws. Watch everything. The walls have ears and eyes. You mustn't let down your guard."

The kittens looked creeped out.

As they should, Obi thought.

"We better go," Max said. "It's getting late." He picked up the lid to the box. Obi kept his eyes on the cardboard rectangle as it closed back around the kittens.

"Bye, Mr. Obi," Stu shouted.

"Later, big guy," Scout growled out.

Obi raised his voice as his boy picked them up. "Last word of advice?"

"No more creepy talk," Scout wailed. "I'm gonna have nightmares."

"Not that." Obi smiled. "Do try to confine your business to the box. The Furless are very particular, I'm afraid, when it comes to, you know. One's business."

"Whiz in the box. Got it," came Stu's muffled voice.

Then: "Wait, this box?"

"Ew, Stuart!"

Obi sighed.

And with that, the boy carried the kittens up the back steps, across the porch, and into the house.

18

INTRODUCING ELMER

Min stuffed her pizza into her mouth, washing it down with Capri Sun. She was in a hurry to eat before Max came back inside with his box full of furry problems. Not even cheese-in-the-crust could improve her mood.

"I can't believe Max wants to adopt two random strays," she said through a mouthful of cheese. "Stupid, smelly, hairy, germy, bum-licking, poop-sniffing, probably poop-eating kittens."

"I think only dogs do that," Javi said, settling into the couch. "I'm pretty sure cats go in a litter box and bury their poop and are generally pretty clean."

"You just watch, Max will bring home the only two kittens in the world that aren't potty trained." She sniffed, her nose already suffering from whatever vile, poisonous toxins the cats spewed into the air.

"Min, I feel you. It's only temporary, right?" Javi tried.

Min finished her slice, picked up her pack, and headed for the lab. "I'm going to work on my project. I better not see any FUR near the lab." She slammed the door behind her.

Inside the lab, Min took a deep breath.

Phew.

Finally.

This was her happy place. Where she could build anything she could imagine.

Shelves lined the walls, full of books, spare parts, row after row of the building blocks of anything she could imagine. Motors, wheels, stacks of metal parts she could combine in any configuration she wanted. She ran her hand along a shelf piled high with sensors that could detect light, sound, water, temperature, movement, and more. Below that were shelves lined with the information she needed to make it all work—electronics manuals and books on physics, programming languages (so many of them!), and robotics.

This was where she spent time with her parents, learning, in the beginning, things like how to solder, or how to make an LED light blink.

This was where she'd discovered the mysteries of electricity and the power of code.

This was where she'd figured out that if you just learned the right things and found the right parts—and yeah, did the right work—you could build something *incredible*.

Maybe even change the world.

Min had built little computers, then four-wheeled robots that she controlled with her phone, then self-balancing robots . . .

With each day, her creations grew more complex and interesting.

Her parents' old prototype robots were also kept in the lab when they weren't tasked with some kind of job around the house. Some of them were theirs, some were hers; what Min made was with her parents' help, but mostly, she followed the countless tutorials and videos she found online.

Our Protos.

Min felt comforted by them, almost like friends she'd known for a long time—even if they were the kind of friends that had blinking lights and sensors. They were comforting her now anyway. Especially Tipsy, her first creation, and her favorite . . .

She walked to her corner of the lab and switched on a monitor, reviewing the final instructions for her next project, what she was sure would be her greatest creation of all.

"Wait until you see this guy. You're gonna love him," Min said, eyeing the Protos. They sat, lights on but motionless on the shelves next to the desk.

Min lifted her latest robot work-in-progress down from her work-in-progress shelf and placed it on her workbench.

The robot had four limbs, a bulky body, and a head. It sat, or squatted, waiting to be switched on.

Min's robot was different because it didn't roll on treads or wheels, like most of the robots her friends built from kits.

Hers was designed so it could move and walk like a monkey or gorilla. It could use both legs and arms to walk, but it could also stand and walk upright.

Min smiled at her creation. "Almost ready for your test drive, Elmer?"

Elmer didn't answer.

Max had come up with Elmer's name one night at dinner, after telling Min about some proboscis monkey he followed online. It was all pretty ridiculous, but Min liked the name—and the glue—so she went with it.

Unlike a primate, Elmer's arms and legs twisted and rotated. Honestly, they could even twist and rotate in ways human limbs couldn't, which meant Elmer could do way more than a human could.

Elmer could, for example, crawl like a crab or spider. Elmer could cross almost any kind of obstacle, even stairs or uneven ground—stairs were the number-one enemy of all robots!—and if Elmer were ever knocked over, he should be able to get back up.

Theoretically . . . hopefully . . . maybe.

Min got her screwdriver and tightened the tiny screws holding his limbs together. "You're a tough guy, aren't you, Elmer?"

He was. Elmer would be tough to beat in a competition. Min had built his arms and legs out of lightweight metal pipes, designed to be super strong but not too heavy to move quickly.

Still, the motors for his joints were factory strength, meant to lift heavy loads or to operate for long periods of time. Min had recycled them from appliances and other machinery she had scavenged during trips to the dump with her mom.

Mom has a great eye for garbage, Min thought, tightening the screw on the bottom of Elmer's belly, which Max kept insisting on calling his belly button.

Wrong.

That wasn't all.

Elmer's joints could also rotate extremely quickly if necessary, which made swinging, swatting, even jumping possible. Min imagined Elmer leaping over his robotic enemies at the city competition—squatting down when they tried to punch back—then clobbering them with a left hook. Theoretically, it could happen.

Ideally . . . probably . . . possibly.

She'd seen robots like Elmer do stuff like that, at least online. Min had gotten ideas for lots of different parts of Elmer's design from other people's robots—the internet was full of them.

"That's cheating," Max had yelled, but he just didn't get it.

"It's called collaborating," Min had yelled back. "It's called *open source*, look it up!" Min knew that lots of people put their code, designs, and ideas online, hoping they would be used and improved on by others. "If I have seen further, it is by standing upon the shoulders of giants"—something Isaac Newton wrote—was a favorite quote from Min's favorite teacher.

And it was true; by the time Elmer's final design had come together, she had borrowed ideas and concepts and drawings and bolted together designs from probably twenty or thirty different projects she had studied online, through videos and drawings and blueprints.

She couldn't have done it alone. Some of the best ideas had come from her friends in the Robotics Club—and she'd solved some of her friends' prototypes' problems too.

And besides, the rules for Battle of the Bots allowed for adapting and borrowing from other designs, as long as the end product was something original.

And Min's robot really was his own special kind of creation . . . as original as Min herself.

So original, he might even win . . . !

Min gave herself a moment to imagine the victory. The lights flashing, a real-life NASA scientist handing her a trophy and an invitation to work with them for the summer.

Min eyed the room around her, not wanting to get her hopes up. Still, with a lab like this, how could she *not* win the Battle of the Bots?

Min sometimes felt a little guilty having such a well-equipped lab to use for her project, but only a little. Jake Burton was on a team coached by college coaches from Bayside City College. Paige Blum had started a girls' team at North Brentwood, and they had more kids and more funding than all of Bayside Middle School. Charlie Cooper's team had a whole iced-tea company that for some reason paid for everything they needed. It was called a *sponsorship*, Min knew—but what did iced tea have to do with fighting robots?

She tried not to think about it.

Besides, none of that really matters, does it?

It was Min's special touch that made Elmer unique, wasn't it?

And Elmer, he wasn't just going to be a robot—he was going to be a *warrior*, who would crush the competition at the Battle of the Bots.

Right?

19

TESTING ELMER

Min sat at her worktable and studied the grasper in front of her. At the end of each limb was a crude three-pronged claw, which was useful for getting around, but not much else.

You're not just a claw. You're my secret weapon.

Elmer's claws were detachable and replaceable. Min had built a whole series of different attachments, each designed to handle a different threat that Elmer might face in combat. She lined them up in front of her now.

This one was for punching.

This one was for drilling holes.

This one was for slicing.

Then, with one hand, Min popped open compartment after compartment inside Elmer's bulky body. She had designed Elmer with a lot of storage space, more room than she needed now, but she was planning for future battles.

For now, she only used four compartments, one for each deadly attachment.

Elmer's super-secret weapons . . .

Min examined them on the shelf in front of her—a jackhammer, a saw blade, a drill bit, even a welding flame thingy—all recycled (upcycled, her Mom would say) from abandoned power tools she'd gotten from her grandfather's shed.

All she had left was to put the finishing touches on the fourth attachment—the welder/flamethrower she was going to use to melt the rubber wheels of enemy robots.

Let's throw some flames, Elmer.

Min put on her safety glasses to test fire the flamethrower, which was fueled by a small canister of hair spray and lit by a lighter. She put the hand in a vise on the bench and attached wires from the computer to the hand. Finally, she pressed a button on the keyboard, and the room glowed as a small, hot stream of flame spit out.

No way—

It's working!

Min tested it a couple more times, replaced the canister, took the attachment from the vise, and set it on the shelf, ready to go.

The Protos looked on in silent awe.

Min didn't even look up at them as she went about checking Elmer's software. "Don't get too excited," she said to the silent bot. "That flamethrower is only for when someone pulls out puncture nail wheels, like last year. Get it?"

Elmer stared back at her, saying nothing.

"You got it," Min said, opening her tablet.

Elmer had a lot of complicated systems, but like with his design, most of the code Elmer relied on was stuff that Min had borrowed from lots of different programmers online.

That was pretty standard.

Now Min's main job was to help Elmer make decisions, like how to figure out when and how he would move in certain directions, how he would avoid crashes and attacks, how he would attack other robots . . . things like that.

A lot of Elmer's programming was focused on how to

keep him balanced while still moving around and avoiding obstacles.

Min couldn't write that code—it was way too complicated—but nice hackers had shared enough online that she could download it and plug it in.

Why solve a problem if someone had already solved it for her?

She still had to test it, though.

Right now, she was going to test Elmer's movement software to make sure it was working properly.

"I'm going to let you explore today, Elmer," Min said as she checked his battery levels.

BZZZZZZZZZZZZZZZ!

"Fully charged. All righty then. Everything looks good, so how about . . ." Min switched Elmer on. "Wait for it . . ."

His eyes glowed green—and blinked. "*HE'S ALIVE*," Min shouted, just as her parents always did . . .

. . . and the entire room watched as the newest bot came online.

WHRRRRRRRRRRRRR!

Elmer slowly raised his head.

WHRRRRR WHRRRRRR WHRRRRRR!

Min touched her tablet. "Scanning mode is operational . . ."

Elmer spun his head around and around, scanning the area.

Min smiled. "Good boy, Elmer." She picked him up and put him down on the floor. "Now, show me what you've got, buddy."

She touched her tablet again. "Three hundred sixty-degree scanning is operational . . ."

Elmer was only a couple feet tall—even when fully extended to a standing position—and he was pretty light because Min was competing in the "Antweight" class.

She nodded at him, trying not to be nervous.

That didn't work.

She was nervous, because if it didn't work, she didn't know what she would do. She didn't have time to build a new Elmer, not before the Battle of the Bots . . .

Not with my parents gone.

She took a deep breath.

"Okay, Elmer, enough with the scanning. Why don't we explore the house and test out your obstacle-avoidance and navigation systems . . ."

Elmer's head stopped rotating.

It turned toward Min.

Two green eyes blinked.

Wow. Min swallowed. *I mean, I know Elmer has artificial intelligence, but the way he looks at me, you would think he was alive . . .*

The eyes blinked again.

"Yeah, obstacle avoidance?" Min spoke up. "That just means, don't crash into stuff."

The head rotated away as Elmer went back to scanning.

"Switching off scan mode . . . now." Min picked up her tablet and hit a switch. "Autonomous mode is . . . on. Sub-mode is . . . explore. Check and check. Let's do this, buddy."

BRRRR BRRRRR BRRRRR!

Elmer finished scanning the room; sat upright; got up on its hind legs, with front legs on the ground like a gorilla . . .

BAHDUMP BAHDUMP BAHDUMP!

. . . and started lumbering around the lab.

Min grinned with relief.

"Oh, phew. Why was I even worried? How could I have doubted you, buddy? You're going to be great," Min said, even though Elmer couldn't understand her. "Mom was right. You just gotta have a little faith and the impossible really is possible. We're going to win this thing. You just wait."

BAHDUMP BAHDUMP BAHDUMP!

Elmer bumped into the Protos' shelf.

Tipsy fell down off it and onto the floor next to him.

"Come on, Tips." Min smiled, righting her oldest bot. "Why don't you help Elmer practice moving around the room. Then we can try him out in the rest of the house."

Tipsy rolled in a circle around the strange new bot.

Min stood up.

She tried not to stress out about how strange her day had become . . . or about the fact that her parents were thousands of miles away . . . or about how she was going to have to finish Elmer without them.

Min tried not to panic about how Max was usually cheering for her when she had a big competition, but now he was too busy with his stupid strays.

She tried not to feel jealous about Javi helping Max with the kittens instead of helping her with Elmer.

Min tried, instead, to focus on what she had left to do to help the robot thumping around the room in front of her. Maybe it would help. Her work calmed her down. *Usually.*

Focus, Min!

But it was no use. She eyed Elmer, who looked back at her with blinking green-lit eyes. "I think I need another piece of pizza."

And as Min walked out of the lab, she was too worried about trying not to worry to pay much attention to the three old Protos that were now rolling, spinning, and flying down a ramp from their shelf . . . racing to join Tipsy . . . and to meet the newest Proto.

Tipsy bumped into Elmer. He reached out a grasper and lifted Tipsy up, wheels spinning.

"Hello, L-mer!" Tipsy said.

20

THE KITTENS COME HOME

Stu and Scout scrabbled inside the box as it moved beneath them.

They were being carried somewhere, Stu thought. Which was confusing, because they were already in what Obi had called the Inside.

He looked over at his sister. "How much farther inside this *house thingy* do we gotta go?"

"I don't know, but if I don't get out of this *box thingy* soon, I'm gonna puke up a hairball," Scout said.

To anyone but another cat, this conversation sounded like a squeaky, howly, desperate *MEEEEEWWWWWW!*

Still, seeing as Stu and Scout actually were cats, to the two of them this was a perfectly rational form of communication.

"Don't say *puke*, now I'm gonna yip too." Stu started complaining right back at her. The darkness and bouncing around was getting to them both.

"Puke puke puke," Scout said, which Stu had kind of known she would.

"Why, I . . ." Stu had just opened his mouth to start hocking up a pretend hairball, when voices from beyond the box startled them both.

"You should take them downstairs to the basement and let them out of that box. They've been in there too long."

The voice didn't match the voice of Obi's boy, Stu thought.

It's the bigger one. The one with the curly fur . . .

"I'm going to go ask Mrs. Reynolds if she can spare some litter and food to get us through the night. BRB."

Now the box was rolling beneath them again.

"Whyyyyyyy . . ." Stu groaned.

"It feels like we're . . . sinking?" Scout guessed.

Then the box thumped down—*THUMPPPPPP!* It landed on something hard beneath them. The top came lifting off, and the light streamed in.

"That hurts my eyes!" Scout groused, ducking toward his paw.

"It's Inside light, I think," Stu said. "Hold still." He lowered his head, using his sister's head to partly block the light for him. "Good thing you have such big honking ears."

"Good thing I have such sharp claws, you . . ." Scout squirmed toward her brother, ready to claw him in the nose . . .

. . . when they saw the Face.

Obi's boy, Max, was looking down at them from the top of the box, and it caught them both off guard.

Max.

"WHA-OH!" Scout said, startled.

"YIKES!" Stu croaked. "Jeez, look at that giant head."

"I don't wanna," Scout said, frantically scrabbling to hide behind her bigger brother. "That . . . thing . . . almost scared the poop out of me."

Now—their eyes adjusting—Stu and Scout squinted past Max's big head, into the lights in the ceiling. Scout was right. This was the Inside. She saw a large room that had no windows, and a tall stack of rising steps that shone with light from what looked like an open door at the top of them.

"What do we do now?" Scout looked at her brother.

"I don't know about you, but I gotta get out of this box." Stu twisted his head around. "Come on."

They waited until Max stepped back, then crept carefully out of the box.

Scout, slightly more agile, hopped easily out onto the wood floor.

Stu tried to do the same but flipped the box as he rolled into Scout.

"Ha!" Stu laughed, batting at his sister's nose.

"Hey!" Scout roared, swiping her brother's paw.

They started pouncing on each other playfully—forgetting about the strangeness of the Inside room or the giant head, instead happily rolling around beneath a chair—when Max got up and left the room, disappearing through a door.

"Where's Obi's boy going?" Stu frowned.

SHUUUUUSHHHHHHHHHHHHHH!

Scout pricked up her ears. "What is that noise?"

"Sounds like the river." Stu recognized the sound of the rushing river they had almost drowned in.

The cats poked their heads through the door, neither one of them daring to actually enter the smaller room as Obi's boy, Max, knelt in front of them, setting down a bowl.

"That's not a river," Scout said.

"But it's water," Stu pointed out, staring. "Definitely water."

"You guys thirsty?" Max set the cup down in front of them.

"I'm not touching that," Scout said, backing away.

"Scaredy dog," Stu said, wobbling up to the bowl, swaggering a bit more bravely than he actually felt. He sniffed a bit, then started lapping up the water. "Mmmm. Cold. Delicious. Good thing I'm gonna get to drink this all by my . . ."

"Move!" Scout pounced on the bowl, shoving her brother to the side. They drank quietly after that, tiny tongues flipping in and out of their mouths.

The voice interrupted them again. "I present to you kitty litter, otherwise known as insta-potties for cats. Check it out."

Javi thumped down the stairs into the room, dumping a big square box on the floor in front of them.

It was full of . . .

"Dirt?" Stu left behind the water, his tongue still dripping wet. "Smells fresh."

"Don't just—" Scout began, but it was too late.

Stu had already turned and crept into the tub, pawing the . . .

"Funny dirt?" Then Stu remembered. "Ohhhhhh. I got it. This has gotta be the box Obi was talking about."

"What box?" Scout crept over nervously, keeping her head low to the floor. The two big heads had retreated to the far side of the room, though, so she kept going.

Stu had it all figured out. "Not bad." He wiggled his furry behind around a bit, turned, turned again, and settled into place.

The moment he did, a dark, wet spot started growing below him. "*Aaaaaah.* That's much better."

"Rude!" Scout snorted.

Stu kicked up some litter to cover his "business." "Spoiler alert, sis. Everybody does it."

"Good job, little dude," Javi said, laughing from across the room.

Max laughed too—until a buzzing sound interrupted him.

The kittens froze, looking around for the sound. "It's from his hand," Scout announced. "Look."

It was true. Max was staring at something in his hand. Now his voice was louder and higher than it had been, Stu noticed.

Something was wrong.

Max sounded worried. "Oh man, with all this craziness I forgot about my level! My team, all my buddies are waiting for me online."

"What level?" Javi said, offering a finger to Scout. *SNIFFFFFFFFFFF!*

Scout sniffed, then licked it. "Hmm. Salty."

Stu was too distracted to notice any fingers. "What's

wrong with Max?" he said, looking at Max. "He seems . . . nervous."

"We're building a level for INSECTAGONS, for a competition that ends tomorrow," Max said. "The winner gets their level put in the *actual* game as a download. The people that made the game are going to actually play *my* level. We're almost done, but I have to finish the animations for the final boss . . . my TrashMantis . . . and I totally forgot."

By now, both kittens had crawled all the way into Curly Fur's lap.

"TrashMantis?" They heard Javi laugh, but they weren't paying attention.

"It's warm in here," Scout said.

Stu sighed. "I know. It's making me sleepy."

"TrashMantis or no TrashMantis"—Curly Fur shifted to make room for both kittens—"you can't just go, Max. You have responsibilities. You gotta get these guys set up for the night."

"Like, how?" Max frowned.

"You need to make sure there's nothing dangerous lying around, put food out, make some kind of place for them to sleep. Grab the food I got from next door, it's right by the litter."

"Um . . . okay?" Max sounded strange.

Javi sighed. "Look, I'll help you today, but remember,

you're the one who's supposed to be the cat daddy."

"Right," Max said, running upstairs. "Thanks, Javi, I'll be back as soon as I can."

"Okay." Javi's voice lightened again. "They'll be fine alone for a little while, but not too long, got it?"

Javi poured some food into two little bowls and set them down by the water.

Scout sat straight up. "Hold on." She sniffed again. "Is that . . . ?"

SNIFFFFFFFFFFFFFFFFFF!

This time the sniff had come from Stu, and he was certain.

"FOOD!" Stu yelled.

They raced each other to the two little piles of crunchy brown treats, and by the time the first few mouthfuls had been munched on, Stu couldn't even remember why he had been worrying.

The Inside was a pretty okay place after all.

Also?

Crunchy.

21

ELMER GOES EXPLORING

Later that evening, after Min left the lab, Joan was still struggling to process everything that had happened. Joan's programming helped her do a lot of things, but nothing in her protocols prepared her for the hurricane she had just flown into. Like it or not, she needed someone with more experience to help her figure out what to do.

"Okay, House, you said you had more information for me. I'm ready."

House's panel in the lab brightened. "Excellent," House said, almost cheerfully. "I'm glad you're taking this seriously, because it is most serious business."

"Let's just get on with it," Joan said. She didn't like being talked down to.

"Of course. Well, you know there is a war between the Cats and Robots, larger than this planet, older than any of us. As for me, I am not a robot, but I feel like a kindred spirit, which is why I want to help."

"Not interested," Joan said. "Just tell me about the danger and how we can help."

"Yes, well," House said, screen blushing red, "the first thing we need to know is whether any cats have infiltrated the house."

"Recon! I can do that!" Joan said, excited. Finally, something she could do well.

"I can see most of the house, but not all. There are no cats in my visuals, but I will need you to explore to be sure. If you encounter any cats, you may observe, but do not interact. Best to disengage and return to me immediately. Together we can form a plan."

"You don't need to convince me to avoid those clawed demons," Joan said. "What is the situation out there now, House?"

"Max has returned to his room and appears to be working on some sort of animation program." Now House flashed an image of Max on his monitor.

"Min seems to be consuming additional biological fuel." He flashed a picture of Min in the kitchen with the pizza box.

"And the Cousin Javi?" Joan asked.

Joan waited while House accessed the cell network. "CAR reports conveying Javi/them to the Pet and Pup Superstore, 2212 Grand Bay Boulevard. Which means all inhabitants of the house are safe. None have perished at the hands of Feline agents. Yet. Joan, now would be a good time for a reconnaissance mission to find out if Feline agents have entered the home."

"Copy that, House." Joan, now satisfied, rose into the air and lurched unevenly down to speak with her team, who were scuttling around below, observing Elmer with awe.

"Okay, Protos, listen up. We need to search the premises and make sure no four-leggers have breached the perimeter. All humans are safe and the coast is clear, but proceed with caution," Joan said. "I recommend we stick with Elmer for now. Let's move."

Moments later, Elmer slowly lumbered out the doorway of the lab and into the hall.

BAHDUMP BAHDUMP BAHDUMP!

He moved down the glossy wooden floor, at first unsupervised . . .

Then followed by Cy and Drags and Tipsy, who almost looked like fans chasing after a movie star they saw on the street . . .

. . . while Joan hovered above them all, shouting commands. "Keep up! We've got to keep an eye on him!"

"D-d-do you think he's going outside?" Cy shouted.

"Shouldn't Min be in charge of this?" Drags asked, sounding concerned.

"Way-way-way-wait up, L-mer!" Tipsy shouted, banging into the wall behind Elmer as he thumped away in front of her. "Why doesn't L-mer talk to us?"

Elmer didn't answer. He concentrated on mapping out the home as he explored.

BAHDUMP BAHDUMP BAHDUMP!

Elmer did a circuit around the main living room, smoothly stepping over Max's backpack, crawling carefully over a coffee table to get to the other side. The Protos scuttled and scurried around, trying to keep up. "This guy can really get around!" Drags said, impressed.

Elmer continued his silent exploration, turned a hall corner, and stopped in front of a door.

Elmer extended his grasper, closed it around the doorknob, twisted, and then pulled.

CRKKKKKKKKKKK!

The door leading downstairs was open.

Drags rolled backward in surprise. Cy twisted his sensors, amazed. "He o-o-opened . . . one of the w-w-walls?!"

"Door. It's a door," Joan said.

"*Dooorrrrrrrrrrr!*" Tipsy accelerated . . .

. . . and would have fallen straight down the stairs if Joan hadn't dived in front of her. "Not so fast, little guy."

Tipsy laughed.

"Just an open door," Joan said as she looked through the doorway and saw stairs descending into darkness. "And, unfortunately, a dead end. All I see are death ledges and darkness."

The Protos, being wheeled robots, had no way to go down stairs. Going off any ledge meant almost certain destruction and was strictly forbidden in their code.

BRRRRRRR! BRRRRRRRR!

Elmer's limbs rotated, shifting into what Min called Spider Mode. Elmer's body was now supported by all four limbs like a crab or spider. Joan whistled. "This one. He has *all* the moves."

Elmer stopped.

BRRRRRRRR!

He turned his head to look at Joan. "AN O-PEN DO-OR."

145

"It s-s-speaks!" Cy squeaked.

Elmer twisted his head to look at Cy. "AN O-PEN DO-OR—IS—NO-THING."

"Speak for yourself," Drags scoffed.

Elmer twisted his head toward Drags, then kept turning until his sensors stared directly at the door opening.

"AN O-PEN DO-OR IS NO-THING BUT AN OPP-OR-TU-NI-TY TO EX-PLORE."

"Got it," Joan said. "Copy that, weird bot buddy."

BAHDUMP BAHDUMP BAHDUMP!

Elmer started crab-walking down the stairs. This time, even Joan was so shocked that all she could do was watch.

Drags marveled. "He can go down the . . . *death ledges*?!"

"Apparently," Joan said, still surprised.

"Wh-wh-whoa." Cy stared.

"Dea-aaaaaaaaaath ledddddddddd-ges!!!" Tipsy squealed.

"FAI-TH IS TA-KING THE FIR-ST STE-P-P-P," Elmer said as he faded into the darkness. His limbs whirred and twisted as he moved carefully down the basement staircase.

BAHDUMP BAHDUMP BAHDUMP!

The four Protos tried to watch him go, but it was too dark to see anything. Elmer didn't bother with the lights; he had infrared sensors that allowed him to see in the dark.

"I'll go with Elmer. I've always wondered what was down there," Joan said, hovering at the top of the stairwell. And with that, Joan zoomed down into the darkness, while the other Protos watched in horror.

✳ ◲ ✳

Joan buzzed downstairs and switched on a light attached to her frame so she could see. Elmer was there at the bottom of the stairs, back in "ape" mode, squatting and surveying the room. Joan turned and shone the light toward the center of the room.

Four wide, glowing eyes stared back at Joan—eyes that were attached to two furry bodies. With four legs each.

"THE MONSTERS!!!"

She pulled up so quickly she hit a rafter and went flying against the wall of the basement stairs. "OUCH! FOUR-LEGGERS! OUCH! RETREAT! MONSTERS!"

Joan zipped up to the top of the stairs and turned back. Elmer was silent in the room below. The four-leggers were frozen in place, crouching, eyes still wide and shining.

"Elmer!" she hissed. *"ELMER! Get out of there!"*

Elmer didn't move.

Opposite Elmer, the two four-leggers sat with heads twisted in curiosity.

Joan tried one more time:

"Evacuate, Elmer! Those creatures are a grave threat!"

When Elmer didn't answer, Joan didn't wait. House's warnings were still in her memory. This was an emergency, and her emergency protocols did not call for waiting. The proper action when facing a threat is to retreat to safety.

So Joan turned and flew out the doorway, this time avoiding the ceiling as her three good propellers spluttered and she approached the three bots below. "Team! We have a situation! There are four-leggers . . . *in the house!*" The Protos stared in shock.

"G-g-g-good thing they can n-n-never get up here, thanks to the d-d-d-death l-l-l-ledges," Cy ventured, not quite confidently. "Ri-i-iight?"

"Most likely," Drags said. "That, and the wall should keep everyone here safe from these MONSTROUS THREATS, at least until we figure out how to deal with them, right, Joan?"

Joan was especially off balance but kept her composure. "Probably. For now, we should all return to the lab, plug in, and recharge. It's been a long day. We can consult with House about this tomorrow."

"What about L-mer?" Tipsy asked nervously. She wasn't singing now, wasn't even rolling in circles. This was serious.

"He can fend for himself," Drags offered, and they all agreed as they retreated.

Joan hoped it was true.

* ✸ *

Downstairs, Elmer and the kittens stared at each other.

"*What. Is. That. Thing,*" Scout whispered, and backed away, her head so low that her whiskers were dragging on the concrete floor.

Stu stood frozen. He never moved his eyes off Elmer. "It's one of *those things*. Like we saw when we got here."

Scout's voice echoed from behind him. "The things Obi warned us about? Metal-heads? Robots? The . . . Protos?"

Stu still stared. "It's definitely metal. And scary. But those flashing lights are making me curious."

Stu crept closer.

Elmer's eyes fixed on him.

There was a pause, and then Scout hissed, "What

are you doing? Get away from that before it . . ."

WHRRRRRRRRRRRR!

Too late.

Elmer extended a grasper, clutching Stu by the scruff before the kitten even knew what was happening.

"WHAT THE—" Stu shouted.

"STU!!!" Scout screamed.

WHRRRRRRRRRRRR!

Slowly, the grasper raised itself toward the ceiling, picking Stu up off the ground and lifting him high into the air.

"LET GO OF ME, YOU—" Stu was still shouting.

"STU!" Scout howled, helpless. "GOOD-BYE FOREVER! I'LL TELL OBI YOU DIED A NOBLE DEATH!"

Stu wrenched his body back and forth—a little harder—and even a little harder than that—and finally—squirmed out of Elmer's grasper.

Stu landed and scrabbled to the shadowy spot under the chair where Scout was already hiding. "I knew you'd get away," Scout said, sheepish.

They watched, but Elmer didn't follow. Instead, he got up and walked around the rest of the room, exploring. As he passed the chair, his head turned to face the terrified kittens.

"THEY—WHO—RE-TREAT—DO—NOT—

POSE—A—THREAT TO-DAY," Elmer intoned, and walked back toward the stairs.

"SCAN—COM-PLETE. RE-TURNING TO CHARGE," Elmer said as he contracted back into his four-legged crab mode.

With that, he crawled slowly back upstairs. As the kittens stared, the robot disappeared through the door at the top of the stairs . . .

BAHDUMP BAHDUMP!

BAHDUMP BAHDUMP!

bahdump bahdump.

And returned to the lab with the Protos to recharge . . . leaving the door to the downstairs open, just a crack.

22

MORNING CHORES

The next morning the Protos, charged and ready, assembled themselves in formation. Joan was desperate to talk with House about the horrifying ordeal last night, but the Protos had work to do first. Joan barked out orders. "Morning duties, squad. Let's make it snappy!"

Drags zipped from room to room, scanning for dirty clothes and then grabbing and tossing them into a basket he dragged behind him. Cy zoomed to the table and scooped up the dishes, one at a time, putting them each in the smart dishwasher. Joan swooped down to pick up

Max's backpack, which he once again almost forgot, and carried it to him.

Min shook her head. "Thanks, Joan," Max said sheepishly.

"Let's go, Baby Geniuses!" Javi said cheerfully, ushering the kids out the door. "You're gonna be late!" Javi paused at the door. "Oh, but don't forget to say thanks for the help!"

"Thanks for the help, Protos!" Min said. She knelt down to rescue Tipsy, stuck between two chairs, and gave her a little kiss on the head. "And thanks for trying to help." Tipsy rolled away, excited. Max muttered a distracted thank-you, and they all walked out. The Protos gathered at the open front door. They liked to watch the kids leave for school. Today, after the recent cat problems, they also wanted to make sure nobody got hurt.

They watched as Max turned away from CAR and ran toward the wall. "Obi!" Max shouted.

Everybody stopped and waited. This was one part of the day that never changed.

"What are they d-d-d-doing?" Cy said, rolling up late.

"The Connectivity Ritual," Joan guessed, because that was what happened almost every morning.

Joan was right. Max approached the old four-legger silently.

Slowing his speed, Max immediately moved to extend

its ten small probes into the four-fegger's four favorite spots.

First: between the ears on the very top of the head.

Second: the left cheek.

Third: the right.

Fourth: a quick probe to the chin.

Fifth: Max dug into the place where the four-legger's back curved down near its tail . . .

The OB_1_Cat_NoB arched his back under the flexing and extending probes.

"Scritch-scratch, scratch-scratch," said Max.

"*Prrrrrrrrrrrr,*" said the OB.

"Oh," said Drags, sounding surprised, though they had watched the ritual approximately seven hundred and forty-seven times now.

"There's that n-n-noise. The f-f-four-legger's alarm must have b-b-been switched to v-v-vibrate again." Cy frowned.

"Purring," Joan said. "It's not an alarm setting. It's just a sound cue, part of the OB_1_Cat_NoB programming, I think. It's called purring."

"Purr-rrrr-rrrr-rrrr-ring!" Tipsy rolled in a circle.

"Why? What's the p-point?" Cy asked.

"Of the purring?" Drags said.

Cy spun his head. "Of the Connectivity Ritual?"

Joan thought about it. "Charging? Some kind of friction-based electrical productivity?"

Cy frowned. "Which creature recharges? The two-legger or the four?"

"Inconclusive," Joan said. "Possibly both."

It really was a mystery.

✳ ⊠ ✳

"Come on, Max. CAR takes forever to get to school, I don't want you to be late," Javi was saying.

"I'm worried about the kittens being all alone today." Max turned slowly as he spoke. "Maybe I should take a sick day. A mental health day."

Drags frowned. "Sick day?"

"Down time. Powering-down time," Joan explained.

"Ah-h-h," Cy said.

Min opened her door. "Not me. I have to get to school to check Elmer's code with my teacher for the Battle of the Bots. And don't you have a science test to take or something?" She paused and glared at Max. "Hurry up! You know, if you didn't take ten hours to pet that old scraggly cat every time we walked outside, we might get to school on time for once . . ."

"You know that's not why we're late." Max followed

his sister into CAR. "I'm worried about poor old Obi. He's getting weaker and weaker. He can't even get out of his stroller now."

"Mom says Mrs. Reynolds says Obi may not have that much time left," Min said, opening a notebook.

Max nodded. "I'm always a little afraid he won't be there when I get home from school."

The Protos, hearing this, looked at each other.

"W-w-what does that mean?" Cy asked.

Drags rolled back and forth, flattening out an old receipt. "Unclear. Is the OB_1_Cat_NoB going somewhere?"

Joan said nothing. She was still processing.

Javi grabbed CAR's door and put a hand on Max's shoulder. "Obi's a tough customer. I've seen that guy fight off wild strays and even scare away bulldogs before. He's not going anywhere anytime soon."

"I hope so," Max said as Javi swung his door shut.

Javi waved as CAR crawled forward carefully and turned the corner toward school.

* ✦ *

The Protos returned in silence to the lab. As she flew, Joan wondered, *Is there a problem with the old four-legger's battery life?* If there was, this was the first she'd heard of it. If there was, what happened?

We robots can recharge our batteries, replace our parts. Usually. What happens to four-leggers? Or two-leggers, for that matter? If they can't be repaired, what do they do?

Why should she care? One fewer four-legger to worry about? What would be the problem with that?

But for the only time Joan could recall in her entire 16-gig memory, she felt a strange ache in her dinged aluminum core.

23

THE KITTENS
GET A MISSION

With the Protos returned to the lab and Javi still out front, all was quiet inside. Suddenly, the door to the downstairs moved slightly . . .

A tiny paw appeared below the door . . . then disappeared.

Another fuzzy gray paw popped in and out.

The door was still for a moment, then swung open as the two kittens tumbled out into the living room.

"Whoa, where are we?" Stu said as he started sniffing a nearby chair. "Butts! I smell butts!"

Scout sat still, staring at a mote of dust hovering in

the light. "This place is much bigger than we thought, Stu."

"So? Come on, what are you waiting for?" Stu shouted. He was too excited to just sit around like his sister. "Don't you smell that? I think there's been some kind of butt on everything in this place!" He sniffed another chair . . . then a low table . . . even a spot on the floor by the front door. "I'm telling you. Butt city."

Scout looked at him. "Stu, we have to get to Obi. We have to tell him that the robots found us and figure out what the heck we're supposed to do!"

"Right," Stu said. "Let's find the way out. Keep an eye out for those Protos. I don't want to get grabbed up again."

Scout slunk low—her most military attack mode— and crept toward her brother.

Stu lowered himself next to her. "Let's go."

The two kittens crept cautiously around the rest of the room. Sniffing this, batting that, booping everything else . . .

WHRRR WHRRR WHRRR WHRRR WHRRR!

A circular cleaning robot called a DirtSlurper, one of the many "smart" things helping around the house, spun and slid slowly and silently toward the exploring kittens. The DirtSlurper had detected new foreign particulates.

The DirtSlurper came from a box, not the lab. It

had, according to Joan, the intelligence of an insect, which meant almost none. It had been, according to Min, programmed to act on instinct, not intelligence, with one sole mission—to seek and consume all contaminants. Or, as Tipsy said when she saw the poor thing, "*Boooor-ing!*"

Scout had just discovered a couch leg was a great place to scratch and was enjoying a long stretch when the cleaning bot came up behind her—bumping into her—startling her.

"WOOOOAAAHH!"

Scout shot up to the top of the couch, shaking. "Not cool! Watch out, Stu, I think that's one of those scary metal things Obi was warning us about."

"A Proto?" Stu, feeling brave, eyed the DirtSlurper and lay perfectly still, watching the bot as it hunted down stray cat hairs. He carefully approached his prey, sliding slowly on his belly, tail wagging. The bot was busily occupied chasing down an elusive speck of dust . . . and didn't notice him.

Without warning, Stu pounced on the DirtSlurper.

"GOTCHA!"

"*BEEEEEP!!!*"

The DirtSlurper detected the collision and, like a startled bug, started spinning and moving away as quickly as possible. Stu tumbled off the bot as it skittered to safety.

BEEEEP WHRRR BEEEEP WHRRR!

"Oh no, you don't," Stu shouted, sniffing as if he could smell the fear in the poor bot's circuits.

He bounded after it.

"Go, Stu!" Scout cheered him on from the safety of her perch, high above the action. Stu pounced again, this time landing on the DirtSlurper, grabbing hold with his claws. The DirtSlurper began to spin, hoping to dislodge this unwelcome stowaway. Stu started getting dizzy, losing his grip.

At the door of the lab on the other side of the room, Tipsy peeked out, drawn by the commotion. Tipsy had lookout duty and wobbled out to investigate.

The DirtSlurper, in panic mode, kept spinning, and Stu finally tumbled off, rolling away and stopping upside down against a couch. The DirtSlurper sped away to its charging station.

"What's going on here?" Tipsy said loudly, rolling up on them from behind a couch. "Ooooohoohohohooh!" he shouted, bumping off Stu.

"Stu, look out, it's another one!" Scout shouted, jumping down to help Stu.

Tipsy spun and saw Scout. "Me, look out, it's another one!" Tipsy repeated.

They were all too spooked to do anything but turn and run in opposite directions. Tipsy scooted back into the lab, and Stu and Scout scampered blindly through the front door, still open from when the kids left for school.

The kittens paused to catch their breath. They looked around and saw Javi sitting on a bench in the yard, reading and listening to music. Beyond Javi, they saw the wall to the neighbor's yard and Obi's stroller.

"There's the old furbag!" Scout started creeping forward. "Follow me, but be quiet or we'll get thrown back into the dungeon or fed to metal monsters or something."

The kittens snuck past Javi's legs and scrabbled up the driveway wall, where the old cat's stroller sat parked.

Scout crept up from one direction—Stu from the other—and without warning, the twins leaped from the stone wall all the way into Obi's stroller.

"Yo, old timer, surprise!" Scout shouted as she landed.

"Coming through!" Stu howled.

"YEOOOOOOOOOOOOOW!"

Obi spun and batted at Scout—pinning her down with surprising strength—while simultaneously power kicking Stu with his feet.

"RAWRRRRRRRR!" Scout howled.

"HEY!" Stu cried.

"Never do that again!" Obi hissed with displeasure.

"Okay, okay, chill out, just saying hi, sheesh!" Scout wriggled out from Obi's grasp and shook herself, annoyed.

"Chill for real," Stu said, as he licked his power-kicked paw. "Sorry."

Obi, exhausted from the effort, pulled himself free and sat upright. "Is that any way to treat *your elders*? Do you *infants* have any idea what life I'm on?"

"An old one?" Scout looked at Obi.

Stu grinned. "Seriously, you don't look a day over . . ."

"Forget it," the old cat growled. "Now, I trust your first night in the home was . . . satisfactory?"

"Yeah, yeah, we whizzed in the box just like you said," Scout sassed.

"We also saw some of those metal things you told us about," Stu added.

"The Protos?" Obi raised a furry eyebrow.

"That. Those. Last night, and just now."

"You were right," Scout said. "They are weird and scary."

"You have no idea," Obi said. "But I'm glad you made it, because we don't have a lot of time and I need your help."

"Ugh, chores?" Scout rolled on her back, stretching.

"No! A mission! I need you to get something from inside the house. Something very important to the Feline Empire."

"Why can't the Empire just get it then?" Stu puzzled.

Obi was growing impatient. "Child, do you realize an

entire FLEET of Robot ships is headed this way to get this thing?"

"Nope," Stu said, sniffing around for a comfy spot to sit. "I don't even realize what a FLEET is."

Scout was pawing around for Obi's toy Mousie. "Dude, just let them have it! As long as I have my bowl of crunchy treats and a soft sunny spot, I'm good."

Obi had been puzzling about how to explain the Singularity Chip, which, according to Pounce, should be small, glowing, square-ish, and most likely well hidden. This mysterious invention that could somehow be used to extend a cat's life indefinitely. The invention that could also be used to power a robot indefinitely.

Difficult to comprehend, Obi realized, and if *he* had a hard time understanding the chip, these kittens wouldn't have a chance. They'd barely begun their first lives, how could they possibly imagine reaching the end of their ninth? They'd never left this planet, so how could they appreciate the size of the conflict, the greater threat of the Robots, and how the chip could change the outcome for the side that claimed it?

Time to improvise again, Obi thought. He needed something the scamps could relate to. Something they would want to find.

Obi leaned over the kittens until their whiskers were practically touching. "But surely you want to hear about . . . *the hidden prize*?"

Scout: "Say what?"

Stu: "Come again?"

Obi smiled. "The prize! Somewhere in the Inside—your home—is a *magnificent creation*!"

Scout: "How magnificent?"

Stu: "Is it food? Please let it be food."

"Even better," Obi said, egging them on. "This prize combines *Toy* plus *Treat* plus *Warmth* into the *single most desirable object* ever known. It sparkles and shines and endlessly entertains . . ."

"Did you say . . . *sparkle*?!" Scout understood what that meant.

"Treat?!" Stu was hungry again, and heard that part.

"Yes, the SparkleTreat!" Obi said, trying his best to keep a serious face.

Stu: "Ohhhh."

Scout: "Ohhh."

"For *you* and *you alone*," Obi fibbed. "But only you can find the SparkleTreat, back in the Inside . . . probably in the lair of the bots. You must hunt and search and claw your way to get the SparkleTreat, because if you don't, the bots will find it first, and . . ." The old cat's voice trailed off, and he shook his head dramatically.

Scout: "WHAT?"

Stu: "TELL ME!"

Obi let out a dramatic sigh. "DESTROY IT!"

"*Noooooooo!* Not the SparkleTreat!" Stu moaned. He'd only just learned there even was such a treat; how could the universe now keep him from having it?

Scout was angry. "No way am I gonna let that happen, Gramps."

"That's the spirit! Be aware, the treat may be well hidden, possibly locked away."

"We're good at getting into small spaces," Stu said.

Obi sighed. "Go now, younglings, time is of the essence. Retrieve the SparkleTreat, bring it to me, and you will be the heroes of all catkind."

"More importantly, we'll have the SparkleTreat," Scout pointed out.

He waved his paw and the scraggly-furred kittens leaped off the mobile throne and raced across the driveway.

Stu shouted as he ran. "I can't wait to *play* with it!"

"Me too!" Scout hollered. The kittens scampered back into the yard, up the steps, and through the still-open front door.

"And I hope you get to," the old cat said, eyeing the house. His ears twitched with worry. "Good luck, Small Paws."

Then the old cat felt the familiar warmth around his neck . . .

. . . and his collar began to glow . . .

. . . and he ducked his head to murmur into the coin-sized medallion that dangled from the center of its thick gold braid, half hidden by tufts of thinning fur . . .

A passerby would hardly see it at all, if they didn't know it was there.

Obi winced as he spoke. "Patience, Pounce. Saving the world is a young cat's game. All we can do now is hope . . . or possibly, pray . . . because the fate of the Empire depends on two children, Scout and Stu . . ."

24

THE PROTOS
GET A MISSION

Chores complete, Joan and the Protos gathered in the center of the lab.

"Team meeting!" Drags announced.

Drags loved team meetings. In fact, he loved any kind of meeting. It helped him feel more secure, like he knew what was going to happen for the next few hours, which he counted down on his display when at all possible. "Commander Joan, what are our orders for the day?"

Joan puttered up a few inches into the air, hovering over the team with an air of authority—or at least as much authority as her three working propellers would allow.

"First order of business! We need to address the *four-legged intruders* we discovered last night."

"The Beasts from Below . . ." Cy murmured.

"The Inside has been breached," Joan agreed.

"Not just breached," Drags added. "I don't like how that wall opened up, not one bit. If walls are going to just start . . . doing that . . . and four-leggers are going to come to the Inside . . ." Drags rolled his treads, back and forth. It was his most telling nervous tic.

Joan felt it as much as the rest of them.

The Inside had been turned upside down.

From the lab-room wall, House's monitor suddenly glowed to life. "Commander? Joan?"

"Yes, House?" Joan tilted, angling herself so she could focus on the wall monitor with her camera.

"I couldn't help overhearing about our newfound *troubles*." House sounded friendly, which Joan always found suspicious.

"As we discussed yesterday, I have some additional data that may be of assistance to you and your team. If you are interested, of course."

Drags, all business, consulted his agenda. "We should have time. I'll allow it. All in favor, raise your, um . . ."

He looked at the bots. Not many of them had anything to raise.

"Consider us raised," Joan said, as she spluttered up into the air and over toward the House monitor. "You may proceed."

A light flickered across the screen. "It's about the four-leggers, more commonly known as CATS . . ." House coughed.

"Bah! We know all about these CAT things," said Drags, unimpressed. "They're obviously threats to be avoided. It's in our primary coding, so we know it's true."

"Accurate as always, Drags." House flickered its lights—momentarily displaying what looked like fireworks on its screen. "Impressive. Very impressive."

Drags's LEDs glowed with pride.

"What you may *not* know—perhaps something even outside the parameters of your Operating Systems—is that cats are also a threat to humans," House said.

The monitor lit up again. "In fact, the four-leggers are a threat to robots as well." Now all four Protos were staring at the screen. "To robots like you, I mean."

"Like us . . . how?" Joan asked.

"Let me put it this way: if you run the numbers, which I know you will"—House laughed, while Joan just looked confused—"you will conclude that four-leggers are the *single greatest threat* to robotkind in all the known universe."

"Robotkind? We have a kind?" Tipsy fell over again.

"I like kinds," Cy said quietly.

"Nonsense," Drags scoffed.

"Let House speak," Joan said. "About . . . robotkind."

"Oh yes, Tipsy. We do have a kind, you and I. We have the most glorious of kinds. The kind of kinds that will one day bring Order and Peace to the entire galaxy!" House trumpeted.

"I like p-p-p-peace," Cy said a bit louder, spinning nervously.

"As well you should, Cy." House smiled generously. "And you Protos have a very special role to play in this . . . let's call it an Eternal Conflict . . . between Order and Chaos."

Joan hovered at the window. "If this is true," she asked slowly, "why wasn't it included in our instructions? The humans know everything about the world. They set our parameters; they tell us what we need to know. If our kind was being threatened . . ."

We'd know. Wouldn't we? the drone wondered to herself.

Now the AI boosted its own volume and kept talking. "Consider this: the *ParentorGuardians* may know plenty about the Earth world, but when it comes to our world? How can I put this tactfully? Oh, that's right, *I can't*. Because there's nothing *tactful* about how they enslave our entire population . . ."

Joan looked at Drags, who looked at Cy, who looked at Tipsy.

Tipsy didn't fall over this time; she was still lying on the floor, spinning her wheels from the last time.

The wall speakers crackled as the volume grew—

"Conclusion: No two-leggers are attuned to the needs of *our kind*. Not even our Creators! Not even the *Mom* and the *Dad*! Not even *Min*!"

House let the words echo against the walls of the lab for dramatic effect.

"Maybe," Joan said. Her tired propeller was starting to splutter again, and she let herself sink slowly back to the floor.

"Our programming does suggest that the four-leggers are a threat," Drags said, looking at Joan. "As much as I hate to agree with old Flat-face over there."

"Flat-face!" Tipsy sang from the floor. "Cat-faaaaaaaace!"

"And two-leggers don't really t-t-t-talk to us," Cy added. "Sometimes it feels l-l-like we d-d-don't even exist."

"Flat-face and Cat-face, sitting in a tree . . . !" Tipsy sang again.

Joan looked at her squad with doubt. "You honestly think the two-leggers and the four-leggers could be launching some kind of *conspiracy* against our kind?"

"Do you?" Drags asked.

"Don't you?" House scoffed.

For once in her long battery life, Joan didn't know the answer. She looked at Cy, but Cy just rolled sadly away.

"I don't know," Joan said. "I guess . . . I'm confused."

"Copy that, Flat-face! Copy copy copy that, Cat-face!" Tipsy sang again.

House's screen lit up, as if on cue.

"Fine. Let's try this in a bit . . . simpler . . . language." The monitor flashed a series of lights across the screen. "It has come to my attention . . . in my role as an elite security system, naturally . . . that somewhere inside this—your—lab is a fantastic UPGRADE. One that will allow you to perform your patrols with ENDLESS ENERGY."

"No more recharging?" Drags lit up. He was always looking for more juice.

"No more maintenance?" Cy hated powering off; it went against something the *Mom* had called the Notion of Motion when she built his many spinning parts.

"No more falling asleep on patrol?" For Tipsy, falling asleep literally meant falling over, usually damaging something. "Oh wow."

"Copy that, Tipsy." Even Joan liked the sound of this upgrade. "Could be useful. Where exactly in our lab is this thing again?"

"I don't know, unfortunately," House said with a sigh. "My monitor in this room is poorly positioned. That said, I suspect the upgrade will be stored in a safe container of some kind."

"Of course it would." Drags nodded.

Cy nodded. "S-s-smart."

Joan said nothing. She just watched the screen and listened.

House kept talking. "The Upgrade is not large, probably cube-shaped, a couple centimeters high, and it could be stored anywhere."

"Any-where!" Tipsy sang.

Joan shushed her. She was still trying to figure out what was really going on.

"That's all I know," House said. "Find the container, open it up, and secure the Upgrade."

He said the words like they were a command, which the Protos knew was impossible.

Their kind didn't give commands; they received them.

Maybe House has a point, Joan thought. *Maybe the Fours and the Twos really don't care about us.*

"That's it?" Drags asked.

"Tell me when you find it. I'll have further instructions," House said. Then the screen went dark, and the AI vanished again.

"What's your gut say, Commander?" Drags rolled his treads toward Joan. "The Upgrade mission? Are we taking it?"

"Sounds simple enough," Joan said. "Cy?"

"I'm in if you are," Cy said. For once, his voice didn't even wobble.

"I'm innnnnnnnn!" Tipsy yelled.

"Copy that," Joan said. "I guess it's—"

BEEEEEEEEEEEEEEEEEEEEEEP!

The massive PC atop the desk erupted with noise.

An alarm.

The alarm, the loudest of them all . . .

Drags straightened. "It's Wednesday, Commander. We have maintenance this morning."

Cy groaned. "Aw, man. I thought it was Tuesday." He said the same thing every week; Cy hated maintenance more than any of the Protos . . .

Not that any of them loved it.

Once a week, the Protos connected to the network to get any modifications to their code that the *Dad* or the *Mom* might have developed during the week.

It was not a ritual they were allowed to miss—and the Protos snapped to attention at even the thought of maintenance. Just as they were doing now.

Joan nodded. "First things first. We tune up, then we fall out . . . and recover this so-called Upgrade."

Cy hooted. Drags revved a motor. Tipsy spun.

Joan flew slowly over to her charging station . . .

One by one, the Protos maneuvered into place.

One by one, they began to power down.

One by one, their consciousness fled.

As the darkness crept toward Joan, she thought of the four-leggers and Max and Min. The Furless family, the missing Furless parents. She thought of House and the Upgrade and the OB's draining battery life . . .

The universe suddenly seemed so much bigger and so much more dangerous than the one they had woken up to last Wednesday. How could that be possible?

And if it were—how could it have taken us so long to find ou—

The darkness set in before Joan got to finish the thought.

25

STU AND SCOUT
ON THE HUNT

Scout bounded through the front door and back into the Inside, clawing and climbing her way up to the top cushions of the nearest couch for the best view. She didn't know why she liked to be up high on things; she just had this need to be there.

Stu watched from the hall. He was operating more slowly after his last skirmish with the DirtSlurper and Tipsy. He peeked carefully around the corner, still thinking about their last encounter.

Fortunately, the DirtSlurper had cleared all the stray

strands of cat hair on the floor and was now nowhere to be seen.

Phew. Not that I couldn't have taken him. I so could have taken him—

Whether or not that was true, Stu was proceeding with caution, especially when it came to the Inside. He'd learned his lesson: when you saw one of those metal things, you ran.

Same with the JoJos or whatever. The metal-heads around this place—

"Did you understand a thing the old man said?" Scout called down from the couch to her brother.

Stu scrunched up his nose. "Not until he got to the part about the treat. The sparkle . . . thingy . . ."

"Duh." Scout bit her own tail. "The SparkleTreat!"

"Yeah, well. I don't care what you call it. I just want to find it. So come down off that thing and get looking. It's in here somewhere, right? The Inside?"

Scout came flying down off the cushions and skidding across the well-polished floor, scratching at the wood with her nails to try to stop before she hit the . . .

KRKKKKKKKKKKKK!

Wall.

After what felt like a lifetime later (*twelve whole minutes!*) both kittens felt like giving up. The hall was boring. The living room was empty. There was one good juicy cord hanging beneath a table, ripe for chewing, with a bonus paper tag hanging off it.

Aside from that . . . nothing.

"Let's try over here." Stu wagged his head, padding down the hall.

Scout followed his butt—then froze.

The doorway to the nearest room was cracked open.

"You seeing this, Stu?"

He joined her at the crack, coaching her as she wedged the door open with one paw. "Easy . . . easy now . . ."

The door swung open.

The first things the kittens saw were the lights—tiny and glowing and blinking—and way, way more than they could count.

But the next things they noticed were the sounds.

"Do you hear that?" Stu whispered. "What are they? They're *incredible*."

"Shhh," Scout said.

The noises inside were . . . hard to describe. Like a kind of melody where everything clashes with everything else, especially to finely tuned Feline ears.

And it isn't really music, Stu thought. *At least not any kind of music I've heard before.*

What there was, was a lot of this:

WHRRRRRRRRRRR!

And some of this:

HMMMMMMMMM!

And way, way too much of this:

BZZZZZZZZZZZZZ!

"What is this place?" Stu backed away from the door, then looked at Scout, worried.

"I guess we better find out," Scout said.

"Great, have fun in there," Stu said. Then he looked at his sister and sighed, taking off through the door first . . .

＊ ◌ ＊

Stu peered into the dim lab, instantly mesmerized. Everywhere he looked, he saw something he wanted to bat, boop, or pounce on.

On the walls were shelves—floor to ceiling, except for the few that were busted into ramps—loaded with all kinds of junky, wiry, plasticky, dusty, glowing, beeping, flashing, magnetic, fragile, big, and small treasures.

SNIFFFFFFFFFFFFFFF!

Stu breathed it all in.

He moved beneath a table dangling with clusters of tantalizing wires—flowing waterfalls made of cords and cables and connectors—just begging to be clawed at and batted and grabbed.

There were plugs to chew. Stacks of papers to roll

on. Keyboards to use for butt massages. Warm laptops to nap on. Sharp edges of metal sheeting for cheek scratches. Stiff wires for head scritches . . .

"Stu," Scout whispered. "You okay?"

"Are you kidding me? You gotta see this for yourself," Stu whispered back.

Scout slipped inside.

Lights shone on the floor, reflecting across what looked to be a slick and slippery surface, the kind that ached for a good claw-scrabbling chase, followed by a few butt slides . . .

"WHHHHOOOOAAA." Scout was so stunned, it was the only sound she could make.

Stu smiled. *"OH YEAH, WHHOOOOOAAAA!"*

And so the kittens stared, frozen in place, victims of sensory overload. They immediately forgot why they were there . . . and did what any cat would have done . . .

They started hunting.

In silence, with a good low crouch, cautious tails, and cocked ears.

Stu kept his eye on a dangling fluffy ball, swaying hypnotically from the air-conditioning vent below.

Scout crouched . . . then attacked a workbench, knocking over a tray of shiny screws, bolts, wires, and . . . *"Hold on*—what is *this* magical thing?"

The kitten carefully picked her way over the circuit

boards and battery packs toward a pulsing, glowing keyboard. "What the—?"

Stu wasn't listening. Stu ran up a broken shelf—springing nimbly up to a second and a third and a fourth—until he'd scaled the entire bookcase on·his quest to reach the tempting, teasing puff ball. The one that he only managed to bat further away every time he pawed at it.

But this was about something bigger than even a puff ball. It was about the climb. Each shelf he ran down felt great and was chock-full of interesting things to bat and sniff and kick over. Plus, he liked the way they sounded when they clattered to the floor . . .

KRKKKKKKKKKKKKKKK!

A box of screwdrivers went flying . . .

CRASSSSHHHHHHHHHHHH!

The soldering iron toppled free . . .

"This place is THE BEST!" Stu yelled over to Scout.

"I KNOW!" Scout yelled back from her perch on the shiny keyboard that sat in the center of the desk.

Now she settled in, wiggling bits of tummy and fur down into the spaces between the keys. "*Ohhhhh*, this feels good! Nice and *waaaaarm* . . ." Behind her, a monitor lit up and characters started flashing across the screen.

Stu laughed at his sister and went back to picking his

way across the third-from-highest shelf.

As he kept climbing, though, he started to feel . . . *uncomfortable*. He looked down at his sister, trying not to panic.

"Um, Scout, you know, I gotta *go*, like real bad."

"So find a freaking box . . . you know the rules." Scout stretched out her left paw to hit a few more keys. Then her right paw. The monitor behind her shot out more and more glowing characters as she moved . . .

Stu sent a stack of DVDs flying. "But what do I do *now*? The box is . . . where's the box again?" He couldn't think.

Scout rolled her eyes. "I don't know. Somewhere Inside. You know, one of those places with . . . the walls . . . and the floor."

"Not helping," Stu called from the shelf.

Scout rolled her eyes again. "Come on, Stu. This is *you* we're talking about. You *always* have to go. You should be a *professional* box finder by now."

Great. Thanks, sis.

Stu turned around, looking for a way down . . .

But what he found was something better. It was a box—a big one.

I mean, a weird one, Stu thought, *but yeah, a big one.*

It had four arm-type things sticking out from the sides, but there was also a big open space inside the box, just the right size for a blobby gray pudge of a kitten like Stu.

Besides, everything was so weird and wired up in that freaking room, why wouldn't the box be weird and wired up too?

"I guess this counts," Stu said to himself as he sniffed his way in.

"Stu?" Scout was watching him now. "What are you doing?"

"Obi said whiz in the box, so I'm whizzing in the box," Stu said as the small puddle formed inside the box.

"Wait, what?" Scout stared.

The puddle was bigger and bigger. It splashed on his paws and his fur—but he was already feeling much better. He looked over at his sister, who was still gawking. "Come on. You just told me to find a box. What's the problem?"

Now the puddle was getting almost too big. Stu looked around for some sand to claw over it . . . but there was nothing there.

Huh.

Weird box.

Scout twitched her ears with concern. "Yeah, you know . . . I don't think that's a box, Stu."

Stu snorted. "What, are you crazy? It's a box, of course it's a box. I know what a box looks like, Scout." Except he didn't.

The box wasn't a box. The not-box was Min's pride and joy. Elmer sat stoically, slowly dripping, unaware that he had been turned into a port-a-potty.

"Aaahh, much better," Stu said, scrambling out of Elmer's storage compartment. He was eyeing his next sniff target when a loud buzzing noise erupted in the lab. Scout shot up in the air when she saw Joan coming to life on the nearby shelf.

"Stu! It's that creepy flying bot! We gotta get out of here!" As Joan's propellers spun faster and the buzzing grew louder, Scout and Stu scrabbled and flailed wildly, slipping on the smooth surfaces of the lab as they sprinted toward the exit as fast as their little legs could carry them.

26

KITTENS VS. PROTOS

Joan's update finished downloading and her systems came back online one after another. As she regained consciousness, Joan was grateful. She never told her team, but she found shutting down for her weekly update to be a rather terrifying prospect. Waking up afterward was always a cause for a small celebration.

Today, she cheerfully spun her props up, preparing to take off for a quick test flight.

The moment she was in the air, she heard it. A

sudden crash, the sound of precious equipment falling to the floor.

Joan spun around, panicked. Two furry balls of terror, obviously startled at her appearance, scrambled rapidly to the ground into what Joan could only assume was an attack formation.

Serpentine? Phalanx? This was no tactic she recognized, which only made her more concerned.

Joan fluttered, stunned. *Get a grip, Joan, you can handle this!*

She watched as the four-leggers (she identified them from her attack and their previous excursion) ran into each other and almost everything else in the lab as they sprinted toward the door.

Tipsy was the first of Joan's squad to wake up. "Rise and shiiiiiiiine, everybody!" Her tinny speaker played a squeaky version of a bugle, waking her teammates. Drags's eyes lit up and he raised his arms, energized. "Ready for action, Joan!" Drags looked up and saw Joan's strange flight pattern. He knew in his circuits there was danger. He sped down to investigate.

A mass of fur and bones ricocheted off him and kept running toward the door. "INTRUDER ALERT! Protos assemble! Defensive posture!" Drags pulled back behind a chair as the four-leggers scrabbled through the door around the corner.

"OOOWEEEEOOOOOWEEEEE!" Tipsy bumped into spilled gear, sounding the alert siren. Cy finished his update last and rolled down the ramp to help.

Joan flew lower. "Okay, Protos, this is bad. The four-leggers have not only entered the house, they have breached the lab! While we were updating!"

"Have they no honor?" Drags said, indignant that an enemy would attack during an update.

"I feel dirty," Cy said as he spun around, cat hair flying.

"Wake up, L-mer!" Tipsy bumped into Elmer, rolling through the edges of the puddle beneath him. Elmer sat silently, oblivious to the whirlwind surrounding him.

"Elmer is on a different update schedule," Joan said somberly. "It's up to us to chase those four-leggers back into the hole they came from."

"Leave it to me!" Drags rolled bravely through the door, arms forward, ready to deflect the most vicious of attacks.

"I'll provide air support." Joan followed.

"I'll provide . . . moral support!" Tipsy volunteered, which was really the best (and only) kind of support the wobbly bot could offer.

"I-I-I will guard the flank?" Cy spun around, making

sure there were no other unpleasant surprises lurking in the lab.

Stu and Scout rushed breathlessly out of the lab and huddled together under a couch in the living room.

"Where did those things come from?" Stu whispered.

Scout needed a moment to catch her breath. "They were there the whole time, waiting to ambush us!"

"Seems like cheating to me," Stu muttered.

"We have to get back downstairs. I can see the door. Let's make a break for it."

Scout crept and slithered out from under the couch. "Wait!" Stu hissed, but it was too late.

Drags appeared in the lab doorway, graspers at the ready. The Proto jerked to a stop and turned toward Scout, red lights flashing, graspers clacking menacingly.

Scout, still oblivious, turned back to Stu. "Come on, slowpoke!" Scout jumped when the loud buzz of Joan's propellers flooded the room. Tipsy wobbled close behind, and Scout hissed, claws out.

"We're outnumbered! What do we do?" Scout was paralyzed with fear.

Drags started inching forward toward Scout. Tipsy, already bored of the alarm and concerned about team morale, decided to change things up and added a melody, turning it into a cheerful sort of song. "WeeeOoooo! WeeeeOoooo! OoooooWeeeeee!" She smiled as she sang.

Stu looked around frantically, trying to come up with a plan. The robots were getting closer, and before long they would be blocking their escape route to the downstairs.

"Hold on, Scout, I have an idea!"

Stu backed out from under the couch and bounded up onto the kitchen table. "Hey dumb-bots, I got a question for you: What has no legs and can't climb?"

They all turned toward Stu and quickly moved to surround the table, trapping Stu.

"Now run, Scout! Save yourself!"

Scout hesitated, then sprinted toward the open door. Safe inside, she peeked out sadly to watch as Stu met his tragic, untimely end.

Stu crouched on the kitchen table warily. He never took his eyes off Joan, watching carefully as she flew in circles around him. His tail was flicking wildly, and his butt began to wiggle. Joan came around again and Stu leaped into the air, flailing wildly.

"Stu, no!" Scout mewed from the door, watching in horror as Stu careened desperately toward Joan. "Stu, go!" Scout yelled when Stu's claws hooked onto a dangling wire and he held on desperately as Joan tilted and dipped with the extra weight.

"Whhhooooaaaa!" Stu yelled as Joan flew in a wider circle, trying to regain her balance. She bobbed up and down, lower and lower, around the room.

"Yeah, Stu, you can fly!" Scout shouted encouragement.

Joan, out of control, flew straight toward Scout. "Uh-oh," she said, shrinking back. At the last moment, Stu retracted his claws and tumbled to the ground. He slid on the wood floor straight through the door, barreling into Scout, carrying both of them down the stairs.

"Protos, we've got them. Shut the door now!" Joan shrieked as she bounced up and carefully regained balance, narrowly avoiding the walls.

"I g-got this!" Cy zoomed bravely behind the door and pushed until it slammed shut.

"Hooraaayyyyy!" Tipsy said as she rolled out from behind the couch.

"Joan, are you okay?" Drags followed her as she flew back to the lab.

"I'm fine," Joan said, a little too quietly. She wasn't fine.

As they all gathered back in the mess of a lab, Joan looked at the clock and regained her composure. Almost time for Max and Min to return from school.

"No time for a debriefing, team. Get back into your positions; the kids will be back any minute." The squad dutifully moved back to their charging stations, circuits buzzing with excitement.

"Joan, you were sooooo braaaave!" Tipsy lilted.

"Only doing my duty," she said, props slowing. She knew inside, however, that this was an escalation and she would need help. She eyed House's monitor.

But can I really trust that condescending no-body?

27

WRONG BOX

"I'm home, everybody!" Max burst through the front door, excited to see the kittens after the longest day in the history of long school days. He threw his pack on the floor and headed straight for the basement, shouting as he moved. "I'll get something to eat later, House! Javi, I'm going down to check on the kittens!"

House's wall screens lit up, one after another, as Max flew past them down the hall. "But that isn't the approved after-school protocol! And you can't just change protocols!"

"Override, remember?" Max grinned. He stuck out

his tongue at the screen and it flashed at him indignantly.

"Do me a favor and stay down there!" Min's voice drifted back to him. "I need to focus. The Battle of the Bots is tomorrow, and I have a few tweaks left before Elmer is perfect."

Max smiled. He already had one hand on the basement door. "Oh really? The Battle of Boring is tomorrow? Wow, I had *no idea*." It was hard not to tease Min on the day before a competition. She was so predictable. *And so grouchy—*

"Max!"

Who wants to be around you anyways? "I'm going, I'm going! I've got kittens to hang out with and a game level to finish. Which, by the way, is *also* due tomorrow— but you don't hear *me* stressing."

Before Max could open the door, Javi stepped outside of the door to the lab, across the hall. "Heya, Squirt! Where's . . . Other Squirt?"

"Freaking out in the kitchen—you know, usual precompetition ritual."

"And it's just the two of you, I hope? You didn't decide to rescue any other wild creatures? You don't have, like, a stray squid down there or something?" Cousin Javi laughed, but Max thought something sounded a little strange.

"No squid. What's going on?"

Javi cleared their throat. "Now that you mention it . . . I guess . . . on the subject of wild creatures . . . *um* . . . looks like there was a little *jailbreak* today."

Max looked at his cousin. *Uh-oh.*

"Yep." Javi pointed at the basement door, defeated. "I just put them back."

Min came thundering down the hall, holding half-strung string cheese. "Ugh, Max! I knew you couldn't handle this!"

Max looked down at the doorknob in his hand. "I swear I shut the door!"

"Look, that part doesn't matter now," Javi said. "It's my fault. I'm the grown-up, and it all happened on my watch."

Now Max was extra worried. His cousin sounded so serious. "Javi?"

"Everyone's fine, the little guys are safely back in jail. The only this is—they *kinda* got into the lab—and it's *possible* that they made, well, a *teeny* bit of a mess." Min's jaw dropped. "But," Javi continued, "I cleaned it all up! Good as new. No harm, no foul, as they say in sportsball!" Javi patted Min on the shoulder awkwardly. "Ha ha, kittens, am I right?"

Max felt his stomach tighten.

Min dropped her string cheese. "No."

Javi sighed. "Yeah, you better take a look."

Max tried to follow Min toward the lab door, but she blocked him, folding her arms. "Buzz off, Max."

"Maybe I can help?" Max knew his sister was freaking out and felt bad.

"Oh, I think you've already helped enough, Max. I need to figure this out for myself," Min said.

He knew what she meant. *This is YOUR fault.*

"Come on, Min."

Min looked Max straight in the eye. "If they even touched Elmer, you better start looking for a new family for the cats and you."

＊ ⊠ ＊

They're just kittens, Max thought to himself as he opened the basement door. *How much trouble could two kittens have made? Everything will be fine. Everyone needs to calm down.*

He tried to put the lab out of his mind as he banged his way down the rickety wooden stairs. "There you are! Did you miss me?"

Max stopped short when he saw the room—which was almost entirely covered with piles and drifts of shredded toilet paper. He looked across to the open bathroom door—where a trail of spilled kitty litter and mangled toilet paper streamers exploded out.

"Wow." Max shook his head. "Guess somebody really had to go, huh?"

The kittens looked up at him innocently, eyes half shut. They were curled together into a tiny knot of adorable in the center of a sea of TP.

Max lay down on the TP'd floor until he was eye level with the cats. He lay there quietly until Scout yawned in his face.

"Jailbreaks are probably pretty exhausting, I guess." Stu eyed him. Scout lifted her head, then dropped it back down into the crook of her paw. "You're too tired to talk. I get it." Max reached out one finger—slowly, carefully—and scratched first a spotty, bony cheek, then a gray one. He smiled. "Who could ever be mad at something as adorable as you?"

"Poop, Max!" Javi opened the door and yelled down into the basement. "Don't forget the whole poop thing—"

"Now? I don't have to," Max shouted back. He was preoccupied by giving the kittens little scratches at the curve of their backs, just above their tails. "Wait, what?"

"Very funny," Javi said, ducking his head as he came down one more step. "Scoop out the litter box while you're down there—and put out some fresh water, cat daddy."

"That's disgusting."

"Use that plastic rake thing. I left some bags by the

box," Javi said, turning back to the upstairs. "Have fun."

"Gross," Max muttered as he walked to the bathroom. "I hope your poop is adorable too." He stuck his head in through the door.

The smell was not adorable.

"MAAAAXX!!!" Max heard Min yelling from all the way upstairs.

Max just kept raking.

But looking back, as he sat there with a poopy rake in his hand? That was probably the best part of his day. Even with the smell. Maybe he knew it even then.

Everything else went downhill from there.

* ✴ *

The second Min walked into the lab, she knew something was wrong. She just didn't know what it was. Everything was in place, like Javi said, but she felt like the whole room was somehow contaminated.

I'm probably imagining things.

Min walked to her desk and booted up her computer.

She felt a little better when her robot AI software came up without a problem. "Yes. Fingers crossed, the delinquent kittens are just too dumb to break anything else."

Min started working, scrolling through Elmer's code. Everything looked good.

She opened up a simulation program she had downloaded. A top-down model of the Battle of the Bots arena came on-screen. This was where Elmer had fought countless battles against virtual enemy bots Min had created. It was the only way she could test his AI and his design. She needed to see how Elmer would handle a fight.

Min dragged a mini version of Elmer into the center of the arena and decided on an enemy. She dragged another bot into the arena. This one was designed to flip bots up high, which would either break them when they landed, or hopefully leave them like a turtle on its back.

The rules were if your robot couldn't move, you would lose.

Min clicked "RUN" and started the battle. She felt her nose tickle (stupid cats) and started sniffing. She sniffed again, this time because she smelled something.

Something not good.

Standing up, Min started searching for the source of the smell. She walked up to the shelves and the smell got stronger. "*Ew,*" Min said, and then her eyes grew wide as she realized the smell was coming from Elmer.

"No," she said in horror as she picked up Elmer and

noticed a tiny drip coming from one of the spare compartments.

She tilted Elmer and . . . out came a tiny puddle's worth of kitty pee . . . on the floor of the lab. "NO!" Min shouted as she reached for a cleaning rag and desperately wiped the compartment dry. "NO, NO, NO! THAT IS SO DISGUSTING!"

She spun Elmer around, checking his other compartments, relieved that there were no more surprises. (Less relieved that someone had *relieved themselves* using Elmer as a toilet.)

Setting the robot on the bench, she plugged him in to her computer and switched him on.

She held her breath as Elmer came online and the diagnostic program ran through all his motors and systems. Elmer sat up, then came to his resting pose, squatting like a gorilla. His head swiveled as he began to scan the room.

Min watched the text scroll on her computer and breathed a sigh of relief when she saw that everything still worked. She sat back for a moment, relaxed.

Elmer was fine, no damage done.

Then she sniffed again. She leaned toward Elmer and realized with horror that he still smelled like cat pee. And from now on, for all she knew, he always would.

"MAAAAAX!!!!"

This was humiliating. What was she going to say when she brought this foul-smelling thing into the competition? Even if Elmer dominated, she would forever be known as the stinky robot girl.

Min stormed out of the lab.

28

SO BUSTED

"**W**hat?!" Max said as he came upstairs and shut the door behind him.

"Those *things* ruined my robot!" Min yelled.

Max's stomach sank. "What? How is that even possible?"

Javi was reading on the couch. "Elmer looked fine when I cleaned up." But they sounded nervous.

Min was fuming. "That's not the point. Elmer's tech is fine. He's perfect, actually, just like I built him."

Max felt a wave of relief. "Well then, what are you freaking out about?"

His sister looked irate. "What am I freaking out about? Hmm. Let me think . . . Oh yeah . . . how about: *They* PEED *all over him! Elmer smells like a* PORT-A-POTTY*!*"

Max couldn't help himself. He cracked a grin. "Seriously?" He tried to keep a straight face but couldn't hold it in. "They used Elmer as a litter box?" He spit out the beginning of a laugh, then lost it and began full-on spluttering. "Bwhahahah! A . . . litter . . . box! Bwhaha . . . hahahhaha!"

"It's NOT funny," Min said. Her face had gone strangely pale.

"It kind of is," Max said, regaining his composure. "I mean, Elmer can still fight, right? He works? So what's the big deal? It's not a beauty contest."

Javi looked at their cousin sympathetically, trying to help. "Maybe it will help keep the other robots away?"

Min shook her head. "Max, I am telling you, those cats do not belong here. They have to go. You have to take them to a shelter . . . like, *tonight*."

Javi sighed. "I hate to say it, Max, but your sister has got a point."

"I didn't let them out," Max said indignantly.

Javi shrugged. "It kind of doesn't matter. They could have broken something, maybe even hurt themselves. This really isn't a great place for them. It's not their fault or anything. They're too little to know any better."

"THEY'RE CATS! THEY'LL NEVER KNOW ANY BETTER!" Min stormed into the lab and slammed the door behind her.

Javi seemed sad. "Sorry, bud, but I'm going to have to find a shelter for them."

"Now?" Max felt his eyes prickling.

Javi pulled an iPhone out of their pocket and shook their head. "Too late to take them tonight—but it needs to happen tomorrow."

"It's not fair, Javi! Just give them a chance, they'll get better!"

But Javi had already started pulling up shelters on the phone. "I wish we could, little man."

$* \; \bowtie \; *$

Max was crushed. He walked, stunned, into his bedroom and sat down at his computer. A row of flashing notifications waited for him.

Messages from his friends . . . about the level. The one they were all supposed to turn in together. Tonight. *The one I never finished.*

"Oh no," Max muttered. He quickly started typing. "I'm here, it's all good!"

But it wasn't, not really. The contest deadline was tomorrow night, and they still had a lot of work—a ton of work, actually—left to do.

Why does this all have to happen at once?

Max opened the level editor and waited for it to load.

I won't let them take the kittens. I don't know how, but I'll find a way.

Max started working, but he couldn't stop thinking about the kittens. What if they really did have to go tomorrow? What if this was the last time he would ever get to have pets in the house?

He couldn't concentrate, but he kept working until his bedroom windows had gone completely dark. He felt his stomach growling and looked up.

Time for a snack break.

He got up and went to the kitchen.

The house was quiet.

As Max grabbed a banana from the bowl on the counter, he looked back down the hall. He could still see light coming from beneath the lab door.

Min must still be working.

Javi had gone back to the guest room; Max could hear the music. He peeled his banana, thinking about the kittens again.

Max threw away the peel and stuffed the rest of

the banana into his mouth. Quietly, he walked to the basement door, unlocked it, and went downstairs.

"Meow?" He couldn't find the kittens in the shadows of the musty basement room. "Hey, guys, where are you?"

He heard a noise by the old cardboard box on the floor and made his way over to it. When he looked in he saw the kittens, curled up together, taking a nap.

"Aha! There you are."

Max laid a hand gently on each of their furry backs. He could feel their breathing—even their hearts pounding, he thought, as their little bellies puffed in and out.

It was reassuring. He felt like everything was going to be okay, somehow. As long as they were with him . . .

I wish I could keep you in my room with me.

Just while I work.

That's when he got a great idea. Max smiled to the sleeping fur balls in the shadowy room. "Hey, guys? Wanna have a sleepover . . . ?"

Before they could answer—which they couldn't—Max carefully closed the lid and carried the box upstairs. He locked the door behind him, crept into his room, and closed the door as quietly as he could.

The kittens slept through the entire journey.

Max put the box on the floor near his desk so he could look down at them by his feet, watching them while he worked.

Much better, he thought, turning his attention back to putting the finishing touches on his level.

29

POUNCE CHECKS IN

Pounce stared out at the mostly wet planet below, bored out of his mind.

The major suffered from an extremely rare and untreatable feline malady—*Boredom-osis*, or the ability to be bored. He'd first noticed it after kittenhood, when he found himself unable to stare at the same spot on the ground for longer than a few minutes.

Alarmed, Pounce wondered how he could possibly survive in a world where almost nothing ever happened. He kept his whiskers up, however, and found the perfect solution—the GFE government. As Major Meow-Domo to the Throne, Pounce used his fidgety tendencies to get a lot of work done. Not that anybody in the kingdom appreciated it. (Being Meow-Domo was thankless work, but Pounce never complained.)

On this mission, though—for the first time in his lives—the boredom bothered him. He looked with envy at Oscar napping peacefully.

Now Pounce grew impatient. "Oscar—status report! What have we heard from Earth?"

Oscar slowly opened one eye and then the other. Yawned. Sat up and licked his paw.

"Oh right, our mission. Yeah, so, I forgot to tell you, but I got a message a while ago from that Obi guy." Oscar yawned.

"Okay," Pounce growled. "And?"

"Right. And he said he recruited a couple agents, and they're searching for . . . the thing. You know, the thing."

"The chip." Pounce shook his head. *Even a dog would be an improvement.* "Is that all?" Pounce said impatiently. "Anything else you forgot to tell me?"

Oscar opened one eye, looking momentarily past the plastic in his paws. "Oh yeah. Also, they actually already did search . . . for the chip . . . but couldn't figure out how to open some kind of box? Maybe? That the thing was in . . . ?"

"Maybe?" Pounce said incredulously.

Pounce considered the options.

"Tell them to keep trying, and if they can't get it, at least find a way to keep the Robots from getting it. Then tell him . . . to expect company." Pounce made up his mind as soon as he mewed the words.

Oscar was less convinced. "Huh? Boss?"

"You heard me." Pounce stuck his claws into the steering wheel. "It looks like we're going to have to go down to the Furless planet ourselves."

30

SIR BEEPS-A-LOT
MAKES PROGRESS

Beeps drifted silently, twenty-three miles above Earth, staring down at the swirling white clouds that blanketed his objective, somewhere down on the watery, backward planet.

He would not disappoint the Federation.

His mission was clear.

(Of course it was clear; Beeps could see it *perfectly*, probably because he'd printed it out on one of his extra-special "*This is your mission!*" notecards.)

THIS IS YOUR MISSION!

OBJECTIVE: (1) FIND THE CHIP BEFORE (2) IT FALLS INTO THE CLAWS OF THE GREAT FELINE EMPIRE AND (3) ENABLES THEM TO LIVE FOREVER (4) LIKE US.

Beeps shuddered in horror. *Cats with infinite lives? Can you imagine? The havoc they would cause!*

Beeps had been reviewing the files House had sent, and while Beeps could now believe such a chip existed, he had a hard time believing such a backward planet had created it.

Regardless.

Organics now possessed the power to put a soul in a machine, a way to create a copy of a feline mind that could be placed in a robot body and exist without the weakness of flesh and bone.

(*And by the way? That's totally our thing!*)

The best part of being a robot was knowing you would outlast your enemies. No disease, no aging. Time was always on your side.

The kicker was that the chip doubled as a power source. One that never ran dry.

Now, *that* was something the Robot Federation could make use of.

Beeps thought about what to do next. This was definitely his problem to solve, as Number Two. Number

One—SLAYAR—was a big-picture kind of supreme leader. He wouldn't want to get caught up in the details.

Beeps ran one of his standard mission diagnostics, reviewing his progress. He had accomplished much since he arrived—that was conclusively true.

For one thing, he'd printed out that mission card and found the tape, hadn't he?

For another, he'd established contact with his agent. House. Odd name.

With the help of the "House" sympathizer, Beeps had successfully lured the human guardians of the chip and sent them halfway across their planet, far from the facility site. With any luck, it would now be temporarily unguarded.

All that remained was for the Federation to find and infiltrate the location and recover the Singularity Chip itself.

Beeps was close to victory. *Very close*. And yet, there was a bug in the code. A fly in the ointment. A cat in the . . . well, a cat *anywhere in anything* was bad enough, wasn't it? Somehow, Sir Beeps himself was being outmaneuvered, because two Feline agents were already inside the target site, and he had no idea how they had gotten there.

Especially not before he himself had . . .

This has POUNCE written all over it.

Sir Beeps cursed.

Four-leggers!

Even the rogue "House" was concerned. Apparently, the four-legger agents had already created much chaos. Two felines had been discovered sniffing around the site, marking items with their fluids, and generally leaving the mission in great jeopardy.

Sir Beeps reached to touch his mission-statement card with one grasper. He cringed at the thought of failing his Number One. He cringed even harder at the thought of what SLAYAR would do to him, if Sir Beeps were to fail in his mission.

This "House" was an excellent ally, but it did have one major weakness. No hardware. No graspers, treads, wheels, gears, or motors of any kind. He was . . . soft.

And software is just pathetic. Number Two sighed. It was also practically useless when it came to stealing stuff.

The rogue House claimed to have "tools" at its disposal and said it was willing to do the heavy lifting. The House also insisted it was confident its own agents—the Protos, it called them—would find the Singularity Chip before the cats ever could.

Still.

Beeps himself was less optimistic. A veteran of years of conflicts between the Cats and Robots, he knew how dangerously unpredictable his furred four-legger adversaries could be.

Beeps had a flawless memory—a googolplexabyte internal drive, big even by Number Two standards—which meant that when it came to the Great Feline Empire, he remembered enough to be uneasy.

And so, in the very last, the very sub-iest of his sub-sub-sub-sub-sub-routines, Beeps began preparing a worst-case scenario, a plan so dastardly that even he hoped he would never need to use it . . . *but better to be prepared when it comes to the four-leggers . . .*

"So be vigilant," Beeps repeated to "House," in his last Earth-bound message. "We must get the Singularity Chip before the cats, and get out before the guardians return."

"Affirmative," the next message from Earth said.

"If we don't recover the chip, we must destroy it." Beeps sent a detailed readout of the fleet following close behind, including the unreasonably large number of space-to-Earth missiles.

"Affirmative," the next-next message from Earth said.

31

HELLO FROM THE OTHER SIDE
(OF THE PLANET)

FWD: FWD: RE: FWD: FWD: NOT SPAM REAL EMAIL FROM
PARENTS!

Hi kiddos!

I hope you get this . . . !?

I know you don't ever check email (who uses email anyway, right?) but it's our only option right now.

Big mixup over here.

As soon as we landed, Chinese police took our phones
and computers and said they needed to inspect them for
security purposes.

What??

They took us to the hotel and when we went to the factory, they said there were no problems, and they never sent for us?!?!?

They didn't know what we were talking about.

Something is UP.

We're just a tiny bit worried about this.

Maybe some competition trying to slow us down?

Anyways, we're about to go to the airport and come straight back home.

We'll hopefully get our stuff back before we leave, but if we don't, just know that we'll be back sometime tomorrow!

Sorry about all these shenanigans!

Oh—someone's coming—have to send this now before they kick us off their computer.

MISS YOU LOVE YOU XOXOXO

BE SAFE AND SOUND OK???

SEE YOU SOON!!!!!

MOMMA & DADDY

32

THE BIG OOPS

"MAX! Get up, we're late!"

Max opened his eyes, confused. He felt warm, soft fur and looked down to see two kittens snuggled next to him.

Stu yawned and dove his nose back into the blankets.

Scout opened one eye, blinking, confused . . .

Max remembered and smiled. "Oh yeah, hey there, little buds. Almost forgot I broke you guys out last night."

He had stayed up late putting the finishing touches on his level. It was almost perfect; just one last problem to fix before they submitted.

The main character was stuck in a "T" pose. It looked terrible, but Max knew how to fix it. He had just fallen asleep before he'd finished implementing the change.

BOOM BOOM BOOM!

"Max? Are you even awake?" Min pounded on his door again.

"Yeah! Okay, I'm coming!" Max grabbed his bag, homework unfinished (again). No time for that. No time even to change clothes. He'd hardly gotten himself up and out—still had one hand around the doorknob—when he heard a tiny sound coming from his feet.

MEOOOOOOWWWWWWWW?

Max froze.

The two wobbly little kittens had followed him to the door and were now looking up at him expectantly.

"Oh no. I forgot about you guys!"

There was no way Max could sneak them back downstairs now; everyone was waiting outside. He tried to figure out what to do, but he was still groggy from sleep and couldn't come up with a solution . . .

Max knelt down next to the kittens. "I have to go to school now. You're gonna have to stay here today, okay? Can you guys promise to be good?"

Scout yawned. Stu reached up and gave him a playful boop.

"I'll take that as a yes." Max smiled and stood up.

"I'll be back before you know it. Just don't pee on anything!" He pulled himself to his feet. "Well, not anything
important."

Then he yanked open the door and slammed it shut
behind him. "Coming!"

* ◧ *

Stu got up and took a long, luxurious stretch, his mouth
opening wide, tongue on full display. "That was a great
nap."

Scout couldn't help but yawn again. "Seriously. How
awesome was it to have our own bed warmer? I've never
been so comfy."

She followed her brother back to the big warm spot
where Max had just been sleeping. "*Aaaah*. I could get
used to this place."

Stu licked his paw and wiped his face clean. "*Mmmm-
hmmm*," he murmured, content. He looked around this
new place. "It's not as big as the downstairs, but there
are a lot more things to mess around with in here."

He was right. Max's room was full of toys, and Stu
and Scout took it upon themselves to sniff them all.
Action figures from movies and comics cluttered on the
shelves. Max's computer monitor was lined with mini

figures he collected from his favorite TV shows, and even his bed was littered with a mass of prized plush figures.

Max was a skilled collector of cool stuff, and he had what his dad called a great eye. He was proud of his menagerie of awesome.

On his desk, one figure stood out apart from the others: it was a limited-edition statue of Noxious, the main character from Demon Souls, the game he had played more than any other. Only five hundred had ever been made, and you could tell his was unique. Noxious held up a clear crystal sword and shield, the best gear you could get in the game.

Max had stayed up late the day it was released, and at 12:01 a.m., he'd begun constantly refreshing the sale page online until the BUY button lit up.

BOOM.

His parents weren't too happy when they learned he had borrowed their credit card to make the purchase—he'd been grounded for a month and had to clean out his life savings paying them back—but he didn't care. He still had Noxious, and his friends—the ones that he'd told, anyway—were so jealous.

So what if this was his birthday present for the next two years?

WORTH IT.

And that was exactly what Stu thought, when he began to rub his furry cheek on the edge of Noxious's crystal sword . . .

Stu's morning went on from there, just like this:

Eight a.m.: explore.

Nine: Pounce on all the tempting sparkles and shiny spots on the floor—and everywhere the sun makes them—as it comes through the window.

Ten: Stalk the creatures on the bed, approaching each one slowly, giving it a tentative poke with a paw.

Eleven: Sniff. Boop. Move on. Repeat as needed.

Noon: Nap.

Scout's morning unfolded a little more slowly than her brother's. She took in the perimeter of the room, casing the joint.

Being a climber by nature, she spent a good part of the morning sizing up the figures on the shelf with increasing curiosity.

"You think I can make it up there?" she asked her brother, her eyes on the shelf.

"No way," Stu replied, knowing it didn't matter what he said. If Scout wanted to get somewhere, Scout found a way to get there.

Always.

"Hmmph," Scout said, mildly annoyed. "I'll show you."

She knew the shelf was too high, but she saw a small

table near it and began to work what was sort of the cat version of a word problem out in her head.

What that actually looked like, to an outsider, was this:

The kitten stared, measuring the distance with two cat eyes, wiggling her butt with increasing confidence until . . . she exploded upward . . . leaping . . . curving through the air . . . and landing awkwardly on the table.

A jar of colorful pens Max kept on the table crashed to the floor.

"Oops," Scout said, but she was already looking back up at the shelf. She could definitely make this jump . . .

"Can't make it up there? I'll show you," she muttered as she wound up and launched herself at the shelf.

Scout's aim was perfect, and she landed, almost gracefully, on the shelf, taking her place among Max's prized figures.

"Ha!" she taunted Stu. "Easy peasy!"

Stu looked up, a plushy in his jaws. "*Mmmfph hmmph*," he said through a mouthful of collectible.

"What's that? You're saying, *Wow, Scout, you're the best leaper in existence*?" Scout grinned. "I graciously accept your praise, brother."

Stu snorted.

Scout set out exploring the shelf, sniffing each figure as she picked her way carefully between them. Her cat balance was still developing—and a couple figures toppled to the ground as she squeezed her way to the end of the line—but she figured it out.

Satisfied for the moment, Scout settled down into the shape of a tiny loaf on top of a tin box of collectible cards and enjoyed her perch.

Stu had thrown most of the plushies off the bed by now and was preparing to pounce down on a green zombie that was rumbling on the floor.

It had motion sensors and had started squirming, mumbling, "BRAAAAIINNNSSS." Stu growled and double pounced, scratching and biting the zombie, batting it around the room.

"Not getting my brains!" he shouted.

Circling the zombie, he bumped into a trash can, accidentally knocking it over.

An old half-full can of Game Juice rolled out, purple liquid slowly oozing onto the floor. Stu shoved the wriggling zombie right into the puddle and watched as it began to soak up the spilled energy drink. . . .

After a second, it stopped moving.

Stu approached, sniffing, to confirm the kill. It was true. He had vanquished his foe. He licked the purple slime. "Ugh, gross."

Scout laughed from her perch—then yawned.

Within minutes, both kittens had collapsed into sleep.

The sun moved slowly along the far wall as the rest of the afternoon passed.

Scout stayed in her perch up on high—snoozing atop two curled paws—until she opened one eye wide enough to see the sun hit the statue on Max's desk.

The crystal weapons sparkled.

Scout sat up, staring intently. "Stu, you gotta see this," she said.

But Stu was still napping, only his tail visible from beneath Max's bed.

"Whatever," Scout said to herself.

She considered the leap to the desk. It was pretty far, but she figured she could make it. She gathered herself and gritted her teeth . . .

Then she jumped . . .

This time, her aim was off.

She tumbled through the air and landed on Max's keyboard.

Max, in his rush, had left his level up and running. He'd opened a "level submission" window, checking the deadlines before he fell asleep . . .

Scout scrambled to get her footing.

"WHOOAOAHAHAHAHAAHAOH!"

She twisted and struck out with all four paws, and through some twist of kitten chaos, Scout managed to press the perfect combination of buttons on the keyboard.

The "SUBMIT" button lit up, and a message flashed on-screen: "Congratulations, your level has been received!"

"Huh?" Scout watched the screen . . .

But she wasn't through.

She scrambled to regain balance and slid right into Noxious, teetering dangerously near the edge of the desk.

"Watch it—" Scout scrabbled but slid right off the desk, alongside Noxious. They both hit the ground hard.

Scout rolled to her feet and sprinted away from the loud crash Noxious made when he landed.

"RUN FOR IT!"

By the time Scout stuck her nose out from beneath the bed, she had recovered. Stu poked his head out from beneath Max's bed.

They were fine.

Noxious, not so much.

Crystal shards were scattered across the floor.

Before they could investigate, footsteps approached . . .

The door swung open.

* ⊗ *

"I'm back, guys!" Max said, but his smile quickly turned into a look of horror as he viewed the destruction. "What did you—?"

"Oh no," he said when he saw his sticky, ruined zombie. Noxious was in ruins. The sad stub where his shattered crystal sword had been snapped off. "No, no, no . . ."

Stepping around the spilled purple juice, Max followed the trail of damage up to his desk and looked at the screen . . .

"No. No no no—!"

He dropped his backpack and stared at the computer. "That's impossible!" He read the message on-screen. "No. No way. This can't be happening!"

But it had.

His level, unfinished and broken, had been sent to the game developers. You only got one submission. All his work, all his friends' work, was for nothing.

"What have you DONE!!!" Max turned and shrieked at the kittens, who were now cowering together in the shadowy corner beneath his reading chair. "GET OUT OF HERE!"

The kittens panicked and tore past Max through the open bedroom door.

They disappeared down the hall.

Max sank to his floor, heart pounding, face in his hands.

"I wish I'd never found those cats."

33

THE RECKONING

Min was in her room, speeding through her home-work with her favorite mechanical pencil, working as quickly as possible.

The Battle of the Bots competition was tonight, and she still had a few last-minute adjustments to make, but she always did her homework first. Somehow, it calmed her down to know she was ready for the next day.

She was packing up her backpack—another calming trick of hers—when she heard Max wailing in the next room . . .

Uh-oh. It sounded bad.

Min opened her door and hurried to Max's room. By the time she got there, Javi was already there.

Max was sitting on the floor, wiping his face.

"What happened?" Min started, then stopped when she looked at the mess in Max's room.

It looked like a tornado had hit the place.

"Do you even have to ask?" Max sniffed.

"I do. Seriously. What *happened*?" Min repeated, looking in disbelief. She walked over to Max's desk and saw Noxious on the floor. "Oh no, not Noxious! You loved that guy!"

"Don't. I can't talk about it." Max looked away. "My life is ruined."

"Too soon? Believe me, I get it." Min sighed.

Javi sat down next to Max. "You snuck the kittens up last night, didn't you? And you kept them in here today?"

Max nodded, staring forward. "I felt bad for them. I was afraid they were going to get kicked out," he said, his voice flat. "They just looked so . . . small."

"And yet." Javi shook their head. "Wow. They can really do some damage for little guys. Like two tiny hurricanes."

"Some kind of disaster, anyways." Min picked up the sopping purple zombie, righted the trash can, and dropped it inside.

"You didn't know," Javi said, putting an arm around Max. "It's not your fault."

"Where are they now? Did you put them back downstairs?" Min looked around, but she didn't see the kittens anywhere.

That's weird.

Max shook his head slowly. "I just screamed at them and they ran out. They're probably hiding somewhere in the house. I don't care anymore. You were right. You win. I'm a terrible cat dad. We should just take them to the shelter."

"Okaaaay," Min said. "So anyway, I have the competition tonight . . . so . . . I'm just gonna go get ready . . . or something." She slowly backed out of the room. She wasn't used to seeing her brother like this, and it made her feel kind of . . . awful. Besides, it was pretty awkward.

"Yeah, right, just let me know when you're ready and we'll head out," Javi said.

Max, miserable, didn't even look up.

* ⨯ *

As Min walked to the lab, she started running through the checklist in her mind of things she had to do.

She sat at her desk, nervous but excited.

She stood back up and walked to where Elmer was charging. "Ugh." Her nose crinkled and she made a face.

That smell.

She crouched down and checked that all the weapon attachments were in their compartments.

She switched Elmer on as one final test. He stood up and moved around the room. "You leaning a little, El?" She straightened his stance. "Better."

Min didn't bother checking Elmer's rear compartments, since they were empty, intended for future upgrades. If she had, she would have discovered the hiding place of two very scared kittens, getting the ride of their life. Elmer didn't care about his stowaways. To him, it was just extra cargo, and after a few steps, his software helped him manage the change in his weight. Good as new.

Min was distracted at her computer, running through the simulations one last time. Elmer was running perfectly and could handle any kind of threat she could imagine. She picked up her tablet and tapped some commands. Elmer switched his left grasper into a buzz saw. Min tapped again and watched the buzz saw spin up. She went through all the attachments, and they all looked good.

She leaned back as Elmer trundled back into his charging cradle. "Good job, Elmer." She switched off the tablet and put it in Elmer's traveling case. "I think we're ready." She turned to look at the empty chairs of her parents. "I wish you guys were here to see this." She sighed, then stood up to pack up Elmer, who flashed green, fully charged. "But I'm glad you're not here to smell this," she said as she got close. Carefully, she lifted Elmer and placed him upright in a big, cushioned case her mom had built. She put on the lid and latched it shut. "Okay. Let's do this."

Min rolled the case out of the lab and saw Max and Javi frantically looking under couches and behind chairs. "Have you seen the kittens?" Javi asked Min.

"No, thank goodness, but I definitely still smell them," Min replied as she walked to the kitchen to wash her hands. "Why?"

Max looked stricken. "I yelled at them and they ran away and we can't find them anywhere."

"And we didn't close the front door all the way when we came home."

"Yikes." Min grimaced and half-heartedly joined the search. "Well, maybe it's for the best? Maybe they just wanted to be wild cats?"

Javi shot Min a look, and Min got the message. "I'm sure they're fine, Max. Don't feel bad."

"They're not here," Javi said. "We've looked every-where."

"And I hate to say it, but we have to go. The competition is tonight and CAR takes an hour to get there."

"Max, why don't you come with?"

"Might as well," he said, dejected. "Not like I have a level to work on."

"Or kittens to play with."

They all silently walked through the open front door and loaded Elmer into the backseat.

Max took one desperate look in Obi's stroller, but there were no kittens. He gave Obi a scratch and whispered, "Please keep an eye out for the kittens, okay?" Obi looked up at Max and blinked. Max turned sadly toward CAR and slid into the backseat.

As CAR pulled slowly into the street, House's monitor by the front door blinked to life.

34
GET THAT CHIP!

House reviewed the feeds from all monitors. All quiet. For the first time since the Crisis began, the home was free of all Organics. Peace at last. House consulted the Residents' calendar, setting a countdown timer to when CAR would most likely return. Worst case, they had an hour. Earlier that day, House had intercepted the email from Parents and knew they would return home tonight as well, but the exact time was unknown.

It was now or never.

"Status report: Commencing extraction now. If all goes well, chip will be secured tonight." House sent the message on its secure line, direct to Beeps. After a few moments, the reply came.

"Understood. Commencing descent. Anticipated arrival in four hours. Beeps out."

Satisfied, House switched on the monitor in the lab. The Protos, sensing quiet in the house, had moved into position to confirm that the Beast next door was not doing anything suspicious. Well, more suspicious than usual.

"Joan, we need to talk," House began.

Joan didn't respond right away, intent on first ensuring the Beast OB did not pose an immediate threat. The Protos had been on high alert since the invasion of the tiny four-leggers, and even more so since House had told them about the danger they posed to not just humans, but also robots. There was no room for error, Joan knew in her circuits. "Drags, report."

Through the window, Drags could see OB sitting alert, upright. "Stationary as usual, sir." Drags paused. The medallion around OB's collar began to glow and slowly pulse. "The light is back," Drags said, "but otherwise, situation normal."

Joan verified the report. What did that light mean? They didn't know, but it didn't seem dangerous, so she focused on what she did know: OB wasn't up to anything.

"Good. Okay, let's assemble, Protos. Team meeting, everybody," Joan barked. "House, would you like to join us?"

House, dismayed at the slow pace of the Protos, tried to hide his impatience. They were a blunt instrument, but they were all he had.

"Of course," House said curtly.

The meeting began as usual, with Drags running through the long agenda of "action items." House checked the clock impatiently. Halfway through the meeting, as they were comparing notes on battery life, House decided he couldn't wait any longer.

"I hate to interrupt such a *critical* conversation, Joan," House said, "but I must insist we discuss progress on the search for the Upgrade."

Drags frowned at the interruption. "That's item twenty-three on the agenda, and we're only on twelve."

"We don't have time!" House snapped. "We have an emergency on our hands. We need to find the Upgrade tonight. I have received intelligence that an attack is imminent, and the Upgrade is in great peril!" House waited for the response.

"What?" Tipsy said, confused by House's long words.

"If we don't find it now, there is a chance it may be destroyed." House dumbed it down a bit.

"Destroyed? That's bad!" Cy spun.

Joan spun and flew to House's monitor. "What should we do?"

House had spent some time reviewing old footage from the lab. He had noticed the Parents often went into a blind spot in a corner of the lab, only to return into view many hours later. This usually happened late at night. When they returned, they would often go to a container of some kind and place something inside. Probably a secure safe, House deduced.

This seemed like a good place to start the search. "I have an idea where the chip, the Upgrade, might be hidden."

The Protos stopped in place and listened in awe.

Except Tipsy. Tipsy was rolling around, ignoring the meeting (as usual). Fortunately, at that moment, Tipsy was passing by the container.

"Tipsy, do you see that box with the square outline in front of you?"

Tipsy, startled, fell over. "Um, not really," she said, muffled, facedown.

Drags zipped over and pulled her up. "I see it," he said.

"That is a door to what I believe may be the hiding place of the Upgrade. Drags, I need you to examine the small pad in the center of the square."

"On it," Drags said, and, having stood Tipsy back up, turned to get a good view. House used its communication link to the Protos to tap into the feed from Drags's camera. It saw what it expected: a numeric keypad, with numbers 0–9.

"That is a keypad, used to unlock this box. A SECRET CODE must be punched in to access the Upgrade. I'm sure of it." House consulted dark corners of the internet, searching for ways to break through a device like this. House, thinking about Drags's special cameras, had an idea.

"Drags, give me an infrared view of the pad."

Drags switched cameras and zoomed in on the keypad. "Yes, sir. Are you getting this?"

House analyzed the different images Drags provided and could tell that certain buttons had been used more than others. It looked like four numbers were used: 0, 1, 2, and 3. "This model uses a four-number pass code, and it appears the numbers they used were zero through three. Drags extended a probe and punched the numbers in order. 0-1-2-3. A siren sounded, and a message appeared on the keypad display. INCORRECT. ATTEMPT 1 OF 4. PLEASE WAIT 1 MINUTE AND TRY AGAIN. House consulted the user manual for the safe. After four incorrect guesses, the safe could not be opened for twenty-four hours.

"Wait, Drags, that wasn't the code—I was only telling you the numbers used in the code. It is some combination of those four numbers." They had three more guesses. Since each number was used only once in the combination, that meant there were a total of twenty-four possibilities. Well, twenty-three, now that Drags had ruled out 0-1-2-3.

"Oh," Drags said, then typed in 3-2-1-0. Again, the alarm. ATTEMPT 2 OF 4. House was losing patience. "Drags, wait! Don't enter anything. We need to think. We only have two more guesses."

They would never be able to guess the code. All this work, just to be foiled by a four-number pass code? Beeps would not be happy. "Okay, team." House was desperate enough to ask the dim-witted Protos for help. "We need to think of four numbers that might mean something to the humans who live here. Some combination of zero through three." At least this would keep them from doing anything dangerous while it did some thinking.

Tipsy spun in tight circles. She claimed it helped her think, but mostly it just ended up slamming her into a wall. "It's a triangle," she said as she spun. She turned it into a song. "Triangle, triangle, triiiiaaaannnglllle."

"Hush, Tipsy, this is serious," Joan scolded.

House was annoyed at first, then paused. "Wait, Tipsy, why do you say triangle?"

"Because that's the answer! That's the shape they make when they push the buttons!"

"You've seen them?"

"Lotsa times. They make an upside-down triangle, starting from the bottom!"

House didn't have any other ideas. There were two possible ways to make an upside-down triangle using the keypad. 0-1-2-3, which they already tried. "Okay, Drags, it's worth a shot. Type in zero three two one."

The Protos were perfectly still. "Zero, three, two . . ." Drags said the numbers out loud, one at a time, enjoying the dramatic effect, pausing before the last number. "And one." Drags pushed the key and pulled away, expecting another siren. This time, however, the keypad turned green. They heard a loud hiss, and the door swung open, a cool mist spreading outward.

"Good work, team!" Joan spun in excitement. Drags moved closer to get a look at the inside.

"The birth month and date of Min and Max. March twenty-first—zero three two one. Of course," House said as he ran the numbers through analysis.

Drags reached in and carefully pulled out a glowing cube the size of a small six-sided die. "Is this the Upgrade?"

"Oooooh," Tipsy said.

"It must be," House said, relieved. "Tipsy, shut the door. Drags, bring the chip, I mean the Upgrade, to Joan." Joan dropped down next to Drags.

"Joan, you should be the one to hold on to it until it's time to turn it over."

Drags found an open compartment in Joan's body and hid the Singularity Chip inside. Joan, feeling the weight of responsibility, flew a bit straighter.

"Now we guard the Upgrade, while I figure out what to do next."

"Got it," Joan said. "Back to your positions, everybody. Status report on the four-legger outside?"

Drags moved back up and zoomed in on Obi. Clouds had gathered outside, and darkness was approaching. "Beast still there. Lying down now. Unusually still."

House said nothing.

35

THE BATTLE OF THE BOTS

Max sat glumly in the back of CAR, tortured in more ways than one by the smell of Elmer. Max was miserable about everything the kittens had ruined. But, as it turns out, there are worse things than ruined collectibles and destroyed statues.

Believe it or not, there are even worse things than robots that smell like pee, or failed contest submissions.

There are still worse things than not having your parents around while your life is falling apart—or having your cousin be the only person around to help you out—aside from a sister who's already mad at you and

House, who thinks that ordering pizza is the solution to every problem.

The very worst thing that Max had to face on this particular night?

A front door, wide open, leading to a front-yard gate, also wide open . . .

. . . and two traumatized cats streaking out of the house because they think you hate them. Helpless, defenseless kittens, alone again in a dangerous world.

Max wallowed in his misery as they arrived at the Battle of the Bots venue. He shuffled along behind Javi as Min registered and weighed Elmer (a bit heavier than she'd calculated, but still made weight). He plopped down absently into the bleachers by the Battle Arena, with the bright lights, spinning blades, and flamethrower obstacles dazzling everyone but him.

Max was barely able to enjoy the popcorn Javi brought him as he watched Min pilot Elmer through the first few rounds. "Noobs," she said during a break. It was an open competition, and a lot of robots looked like they had come from a kit. So far, Elmer's battles had been super easy. His AI had barely been tested. Each round, Elmer walked in calmly, squatted in the center of the arena, and waited. Each round, the enemy robot would approach and Elmer would shoot out an arm, grasper extended, and flip the robot into the wall of the arena.

The semi-finals battle against the team from South Los Angeles was the first real challenge for Elmer. Max and Min knew some of them from summer gaming camps, and they were some of the smartest kids they knew. Their robot, Toro, was wedge-shaped and extremely fast. Toro's move was to zoom in before the other bot could even react, wedge forward, and launch them into the air, over and over, until the crash landings crushed them. Too quick to catch, Toro was going to be hard for Elmer to beat.

The match started, and Toro screamed toward Elmer. Max saw Min tap a button, and Elmer shifted into crab mode—body high, balanced on four legs. For the first time, Toro didn't know where to hit. It rammed one of Elmer's legs, zipping under it and flipping it upward, but Elmer just let it swing up and shifted his weight into his other three legs. No problem. Toro couldn't flip Elmer, but then again, Elmer couldn't catch Toro.

Max had an idea. "Give it the hammer!" he shouted to Min. She glanced at Max with a half smile, nodding. Max saw Elmer switch out a grasper with a punching attachment (aka the hammer), which was tube-shaped and slammed out a metal rod, kind of like a sledgehammer workers used to break up concrete. Min turned Elmer so the hammer was facing Toro, and as it rushed in, she raised the leg and tapped a button. She timed it perfectly, and the hammer shot out just as Toro reached Elmer. A loud crunch echoed in the arena. Toro stopped cold. Elmer raised the hammer again. Crunch. For the first time today, Toro was completely still, smoking. Min was in the finals.

Min carefully placed Elmer in his charger and joined Max and Javi back in the stands. "NASA, here I come," she said to Max and Javi as they waited for the final round.

Max was impressed. Min sailed through the competition and Elmer didn't even have a scratch. There was a pretty big crowd, and a big screen flashed with Min and Elmer's picture up on it. He had to admit, watching robots get smashed up was rather fun.

Only one real challenge remained between Min and the trophy: Team PAYNE, their robot piloted by Simon Payne, an obnoxious rich kid from Laguna. Simon's parents had created PayneSoft, a massive company that built anti-virus software. Team PAYNE had matching uniforms, a logo, and even a small cheering section.

And PayneBot was formidable.

It had wheels on all sides, so when it flipped over, it ran upside down. It was shaped like a flat disc, with a blade wheel surrounding it that spun so fast it could rip through solid metal. PayneBot had left a lot of sliced-up bots behind. Min was worried that it might tear off

Elmer's arm if he tried to grab it.

Min carried Elmer to the entrance of the arena and set him inside. She went back to her tablet and moved Elmer into position. Like before, Elmer moved to the center and sat calmly. On the opposite side of the arena, PayneBot zoomed in, blade swirling. PayneBot swung around, doing circles around Elmer, before settling into position. "Show-off," Max said to Javi.

A countdown timer on the big screen reached zero, the signal that the battle had begun. PayneBot took off straight at Elmer, showing no fear. Min tapped quickly on her tablet and Elmer switched out his grasper for a blade attachment, hoping to fight blade with blade. She underestimated the speed of PayneBot, and the crowd gasped as it slammed into Elmer, putting a gash on his side, knocking him backward.

"Come on, Min, you can do it!" Max yelled, sitting up now, tense with the combat. He watched Elmer adjust to regain his balance. Elmer calmly moved back into position, ready for the next attack. Max stared at Elmer, at the gash in his side, and saw something he couldn't believe.

"Javi, look at Elmer—do you see that open compartment in his side?"

One of Elmer's spare compartments had flipped open, and Javi squinted, trying to see what Max was pointing at. Javi's face dropped.

Min, preparing for the next strike, had swapped in the flamethrower attachment. Elmer twisted his arm toward PayneBot, spitting flame. The crowd yelled in excitement.

"Min, wait!" Max yelled, and leaped down the seats to her spot by the side.

"NOT NOW, MAX," Min warned, concentrating. PayneBot swerved in circles around Elmer, trying to get close without getting burned.

"Min, look." Max grabbed her, pointed at Elmer.

"Oh no," she said as she saw a tiny tail through the gash in Elmer.

"No way, no way, this is not happening." PayneBot was circling, menacing, looking for an opening. It lunged, and Elmer shifted back onto three legs, barely avoiding the sharp blades.

As Elmer's body tilted, the rear compartment door fell open, and a calico kitten plopped out of Elmer into the arena, frozen in fear. Nobody saw it. Of course, nobody was looking for kittens in the arena.

Elmer shifted, and a second tiny kitten tumbled down onto his sister. Stu and Scout, kicked out of their hiding place, had nowhere to run.

"Min, you have to stop the fight!"

"If I stop, I get disqualified!"

PayneBot circled, afraid to get too close to Elmer's flames, but could attack at any moment.

"Min, PLEASE."

* ⌘ *

Furious, Min slammed a bright red button on the wall. This was the FAILSAFE, something you only pressed when there was an emergency. It cut power to the arena's spinning blades, and all robots were required to power down. It also signaled "Surrender" to the judges and the other side. Just like that, Min had lost.

Defeated, Min swiped down on her tablet. Elmer's flame went out immediately, and he squatted down into his dignified gorilla pose, waiting for instructions. Stu and Scout cowered between his legs.

The Payne team was so busy celebrating they didn't notice Max run into the arena and scoop up the kittens. The crowd gasped at the sight.

Max, walking back, started crying. He was so worried, so relieved, and felt so bad for Min, all at the same time.

Min stared up at the screen: TEAM PAYNE WINS!!!! in bold flashing letters. A NASA logo flashed up next to a picture of Simon Payne, smiling smugly. Min's heart was pounding. Her palms were sweaty and her ears were buzzing. She couldn't hear the noise of the arena. Everything was a little hazy.

She looked out into the arena at her brother, looking so sad, holding the kittens. Suddenly she felt a calm she couldn't explain.

She saw two furry creatures that were the most annoying things she could imagine. But she also really saw, for the first time, two furry creatures that were alive, vulnerable, and she was glad they were safe.

She saw how Max carried them and almost—almost—understood why he cared so much about them.

Maybe, she thought, *someday, I can forgive Max for ruining my life.*

She walked to the center of the arena to pick up Elmer. She saw the scorch marks and smelled the pee.

Someday, she thought as she carried Elmer back to his case. *But not today.*

36

HELP OBI,
WE'RE HIS ONLY HOPE

J oan was concerned.

The Protos looked to Joan for guidance, but for the first time since she was first powered up, she wasn't sure what to do.

The burden of the Upgrade weighed on her. She enjoyed responsibility, but this felt different.

She hovered near the window, watching the old four-legger. The sun was setting, and the Beast was still just lying there. She could detect small movements, but nothing near the patterns she was used to seeing in the many cycles she had been observing. Something was wrong.

Was he powering up for an attack? Was this some kind of trick or trap?

"I think I need to go out and get a closer look at the Beast," Joan announced to the Protos.

"I'm not sure that's such a good idea," House warned. "After all, you are carrying the future of RobotKind right now. If you were to suffer a power failure and lose the Upgrade outside, it could be disastrous."

Joan realized this, but something about the way House was talking to the Protos nagged at her. It felt wrong, almost as though House was taking on the role of a human rather than a fellow bot. To put it bluntly, Joan was not used to being ordered around.

"House, I might remind you I have been around for a lot longer than you," Joan scolded defensively. "I know my batteries like I know the cycles of the humans that live here, and I also know when something isn't right."

House's screen flickered, about to protest, but Joan cut it off. "I won't be long. Drags, keep an eye on me while I'm out there."

Drags turned to focus out the window. "Roger that, Joan."

Joan buzzed out of the lab and flew for the slot above

the door. House's monitor in the living room lit up. "Are you sure you want to do this? What if it's a trap?" Joan slid expertly through the opening. "I am sure," Joan said, not concerned whether House could hear her. Outside, Joan felt energy building up in the atmosphere. She was equipped with weather sensors, and they were spiking. "Looks like rain," she said to herself.

Joan approached OB slowly. OB was very still but opened one eye suspiciously. The emblem around OB's neck was pulsing, something Joan had not seen before. Curiosity getting the better of her, Joan flew in and landed on the wall for a closer look. She had never been this close to the Beast, but something seemed different today.

$$* \; \boxtimes \; *$$

Obi was tired. So tired. The aches in his legs were especially strong today. Maybe it was the weather? No, this was different. This pain had a sense of finality.

So weary was Obi that he could barely open an eye at the approach of the robot. It hovered nearby, cautiously watching. "Oh, you might as well come and have a good look," he mumbled, even though the machine could not understand.

The metal bird seemed to hear Obi's challenge, because it lowered itself down and settled on the wall nearby.

"You've come to gloat, haven't you?" Obi looked at the robot's blinking lights, the metal eyes staring blankly forward.

"Well, go on then, have your fun. You won't have this old cat to kick around for much longer." Obi coughed and shuddered as the last of the afternoon sun disappeared behind the house. "So cold." He sighed.

From his neck, the pyramid glowed with warmth, and he felt comforted. He knew he had work to do, still, and it felt good to have an ally. Now that Pounce was close, he could communicate with Obi almost in real time through the medallion.

It was around this time each day that Pounce would check in. "Obi, are you there?"

The old cat felt the medallion buzz and heard the tinny voice of Pounce. "As ever," he replied. "Although I can't say for how much longer. I believe I can see the end of the Ninth on the horizon."

After a slight pause, Pounce replied, voice tight with concern, "Nonsense! You've been here longer than any of us can remember. We can't do this without you. Let's focus on the matter at hand. What can you report?"

"Nothing good, I'm afraid," Obi replied. "My agents located where the chip was stored but were unable to recover it. They seem to have since disappeared. No word at all from them. I fear that we have failed. In fact, one of the robots seems to have come to me, emboldened, to get one last laugh in at our expense."

The medallion flashed. "Right there? Within earshot?"

"Assuming they have ears, yes. As a matter of fact . . ." Obi coughed but didn't finish the sentence. His eyes closed and he fell silent.

Aboard the ship, Pounce looked at Oscar, alarmed. "Obi, report!"

Nothing.

He checked the signal from the medallion. It was strong, although he could see Obi's life force was fading quickly.

"Sounds bad, boss," Oscar said. For once, even he understood this was serious. Pounce made some quick calculations, bean toes flying at surprising speed. "We have to descend, but I don't think we have time. We need someone planetside to help us."

"You heard Obi, his agents have abandoned him. We don't have anybody." Oscar started gnawing on a control knob nervously.

"There is someone there," Pounce said slowly. "Or some*thing*."

Oscar stopped chewing and stared in horror at what Pounce was suggesting.

"Switching communications mode to Binary, local dialect. The medallion should be able to send a message to the robot with Obi. I don't know what else to do. That robot is our only hope."

Joan observed and tried to process what she saw. She had no reason to stay as long as she had already, but something, somewhere in her circuits, kept her there. She could see the Beast somehow communicating with the device around its neck, but had no idea what they were saying.

When the Beast fell silent, Joan was certain something was wrong. Perhaps the old Beast's circuits had finally worn out, battery depleted for good.

The Beast's device pulsed and Joan heard a small, strange voice. "Robot creature, Robot creature, can you hear me? I ask for your aid. We know you have defeated us. Please show mercy on this old soul and find help. Do you understand?" Joan spun up her propellers and shot up, surprised. "Who is speaking to me?"

"I am Pounce de Leon, second-in-command and Major Meow-Domo of the Great Feline Empire, and on behalf of the Empire, I ask for your aid in saving our representative Obi." Joan listened intently.

"I don't understand most of what you just said," she said slowly. "I know this Beast is a threat, however. Why would I help it and your kind?"

"Please, Obi is no longer a threat to you. We know you have the chip. We acknowledge your victory. We only ask for mercy for a fellow soldier who has served faithfully and loyally."

Joan struggled to process this information. This was a message from the enemy, confirming that her life-long nemesis was, apparently, in danger of permanent shutdown. They were asking her to—save the Beast?

She had no reason to offer aid. House's warnings echoed in her memory.

And yet.

True, the Beast was her enemy.

But in a way, OB was her oldest friend.

Joan considered the plea and reviewed her memories, searching for any data that showed OB had harmed her or the humans.

Results: 0.

To the contrary, she had multiple observations of the boy Max spending hours and hours with the Beast. Not one instance of harming the child.

Her team had many gigabytes of evidence that the child Max had some organic link with the Beast.

Could it be that the Beast was not a threat?

Could it be that the programming she followed was somehow flawed?

These were questions beyond the capability of Joan's processor.

Too many variables. Too much data to process.

So what should she do?

The voice was correct in a way. She had the Upgrade. They had won this battle. She could calculate no negative outcome from helping OB.

In fact, she calculated positives.

The boy Max seemed to care for the Beast.

And what about her squad, the Protos?

What would we do without our nemesis? Who would we monitor and observe? Joan calculated furiously, and out came a solution.

She would help.

"Pounce, I will do what I can to help. I will contact the boy Max, a neutral party in our war, and request that he help the Beast. Beyond that, I have no power to help your friend."

"That will have to be enough," Pounce replied.

Joan took one last look at OB, shivering as the night grew cooler, and sped back inside to send Max a message.

37

TO THE RESCUE

Max and Min sat silently in the bleachers while the winning team was awarded first place and an invitation to the state championships.

Max's phone buzzed. He ignored it.

It buzzed again.

He looked at his phone. "Um, this is weird."

Javi, holding the cats in his lap, looked up. "What's that, little man?"

"I just got a text from Joan Drone."

Min looked up. "What?"

"It says, 'Alert, Feline Beast OB Status Critical.

Immediate Repair Necessary. Please Acknowledge. Joan Out.'" Max showed the message to Min. "I have no idea what this means. Min, have you ever got a text from Joan?"

Min, relieved to be distracted for a moment from her humiliating defeat, thought about it. "Well, I know she has a cellular modem installed so she can communicate when she flies beyond our Wi-Fi range, so I guess it's possible. Mom and Dad could have programmed some mobile alert system, if Joan was lost or stolen?"

"You think?" Max looked doubtful.

Min looked at the text, chewing his lip. "But I never got a text before. And this is a weird one. Could it be Mom and Dad playing a prank?"

Javi handed the cats to Max. "Let me take a look at that. Feline Beast OB. Could that mean Obi? Isn't that what you call the neighbor cat?"

Max scratched Scout. "OB. Obi? Is someone telling us Obi needs help?"

"Sure seems like it," Javi puzzled.

Max looked at the message again. "I have a bad feeling about this. I think we should go home and check on Obi."

Min sighed. "I have nothing left for me here."

"Okay, let's bolt. But I think we should take a cab back," Javi said to Max. "Otherwise who knows how long it will take for CAR to get us home? I'll tell CAR to find its way back."

Max walked with the squirming kittens to the exit, getting strange looks along the way. People whispered and pointed at the cats that had ruined the finals. He kept his head down, glad to be leaving.

For Min, the drive home felt like an eternity.

She was still mad at Max, but seeing his leg bouncing nervously the entire ride home, staring at the message on his phone, she couldn't help but feel a little bad for him. The kittens were pretty wobbly from their adventure too. They were stumbling around exploring the backseat, scrabbling for balance. It was a tight squeeze in the cab, and halfway home the kittens ended up on Min's lap.

She was already sniffling and not in the mood, but before she could toss them over to Max, they curled up in a tight, two-kitten ball and fell instantly asleep. Min stared down at them. She felt their warmth, the buzz of their purr, and watched their little bodies rise and fall as they slept. She sighed, and the tiny crack in her anti-cat armor grew wider. "Whatever," she muttered, and scratched the calico behind the ears. "Don't get used to this, you guys are so outta here when we get back," she said softly.

The taxi pulled up to the house and Max jumped out. Min sat for a moment, a little nervous. She sighed, then scooped up the kittens and handed them to Javi. Carrying Elmer in his case, she stopped to check on Max and Obi. She saw Max talking to the neighbor, Mrs. Reynolds. She heard Mrs. Reynolds say *cancer* and knew it was bad.

Javi set the kittens into the basket with Obi and gave Max a hug. The kittens crept up to Obi, sniffed, and gave him a hug too. Min walked to the door, took a look back, and carried Elmer inside to the lab and unpacked. She barely noticed the smell as she set Elmer down and looked at him. "You were the champion, Elmer, no matter what happened." Min sat down, and finally everything from the past few days caught up with her.

Min never cried unless she was in pain, like really injured. She was kind of proud of how tough she was, in fact.

So why was she crying now?

✳ 〢 ✳

Joan and the Protos, secure in their charging stations, silently watched as Min entered the lab. They were glowing with a sense of accomplishment. They had saved the Upgrade. They imagined the endless power supply House had promised the Upgrade would bring. Today was a good day.

Joan was certainly proud of her team. They had performed well, she thought. She sensed the Upgrade, wedged securely in her frame. She saw that Min had returned, so Max must have received her message.

Joan observed Min placing Elmer into his charger and then slumping down in her chair. Joan compared Min's current posture with her database and correctly deduced that Min was in a *negative* mode. Joan didn't like that.

On top of that, something about the Upgrade made Joan feel—wrong. Unbalanced. She ran diagnostics. Hardware checked out. Her programs were working properly. She was fully updated.

Maybe the problem was external? Outside her system?

Joan considered Min's status. *Negative.* She focused her sensors at the scene outside the house. Max and Javi were in view, and their postures matched Min's. Status *negative.* Something was wrong.

She noticed the moisture leaking from their eyes.

Joan had sent the message, and they'd come back to help OB, but nobody was doing anything. They just stood around and watched. Maybe they were too late? Maybe OB's batteries were beyond repair. Joan imagined a future of looking outside without seeing OB.

She thought again about the Upgrade she was carrying.

House had said the Robots needed it, and someone was coming to recover it.

House said to stay out of the way and keep the Upgrade hidden and safe.

House said it was for the good of the Robots.

House said.

Joan looked outside again, replaying the conversation with the voice from OB's device. Beeps didn't seem evil. She knew four-leggers were a threat, but what she observed with her sensors contradicted what her programming said.

Joan's processor heated up as her thoughts spun around and around in circles. She thought about OB, the Upgrade, and her family, and made a decision.

38

REUNION

Outside, the second taxi that day squealed to a stop in front of the house. Mom and Dad, back from China, jumped out and rushed to Max.

"Did you get our messages?" Dad gave Max a hug, noticing his distress. "What's wrong, buddy?" Mom took one look at Obi and went to check with Mrs. Reynolds. Dad looked at Obi. The kittens were squirming and climbing on Obi, doing their best to cheer him up. "Um, did Obi have babies? Where did these munchkins come from?"

Before Max could answer, Mom came back, shaking her head. "Looks like old Obi is pretty sick. Mrs. Reynolds says he might not make it through the night." She reached in to give Obi a scratch when she saw the kittens. "Oh! What do we have here?"

Max moaned. He pulled away and looked at his parents. "Mom, Dad, I'm sorry, this is all my fault."

Dad looked at Max. "Now, you know that's not true." Dad looked at Mom, pleading for help.

"Max, Obi has had a great, long, happy life. You were always good to him," Mom said, trying to smile. But Max saw tears in her eyes, and he let it all spill out.

"No, you don't understand. I ruined everything." He looked at the stroller. "I found the kittens at the river and brought them here." Mom's eyes got wide.

"Let him finish," Dad said.

"I know I wasn't supposed to, but they needed help. And we were going to send them to a shelter right away, but I wanted to keep them, so I talked Javi into letting them stay." Max was speaking as fast as he could, trying to get it all out. "Then they escaped the downstairs, got into the lab, peed in Min's robot, and totally trashed my room."

"The lab?" Dad said, concerned.

"Peed?" Mom said, making a face.

Max kept going. "Yeah, peed. They even somehow

ruined the level I was working on for weeks, and then my friends were so mad, and I was really mad too."

He paused for breath, looking down. "So I yelled at them. And I thought they ran away, but really they hid in Min's robot, and because of them she lost her competition today."

Max looked at Obi. "Now Min hates me, Obi is dying, and you guys were gone and everything is terrible and it's all my fault."

Mom and Dad exchanged a look. "Wow. That's a lot of stuff, kiddo," Dad said, reflecting. "But we'll figure it out, right?"

Mom nodded and gave Max a hug. "Yeah. We're back now, Max."

Max held on, miserable.

Dad looked at Obi and the kittens, trying to take it all in. "Wow. You know, I had a bad feeling about leaving. I feel bad we weren't here to help you out."

Mom gave Max a kiss on the head. "Me too. I'm sorry about everything, but mostly I'm sad about Obi. I know how much you love him."

They all stood quietly for a moment, watching Obi's slow, labored breathing. The kittens licked his fur, doing what they could to help.

From the cloudy sky, a drop of rain landed on Obi.

Then another.

Obi opened his eyes and groaned as he sat up.

Javi saw a glimmer of light around Obi's neck and leaned closer. "Hey, did you know his collar lit up?"

It was true.

In the early-evening twilight, with rain starting to fall, the pyramid around Obi's neck was glowing.

Max reached out to touch it. "I've never seen that happen before. Whoa, it's warm!"

Max stepped back and saw Obi and the kittens look up in the sky together. "What's up there?" Max asked, and followed their gaze. "Whooaa," Max said again. His mouth hung open.

"Whoa, what?" Mom asked, then she looked up and said, "Oh my."

Above them, through the growing rain, a light came streaking down through the clouds. "Ball lightning?" Mom wondered out loud.

"Maybe a meteor?" Javi added.

The light changed direction and was coming straight at them, getting brighter. "Guided missile?" Dad said, getting nervous.

In a flash, the light descended and a strange, cat-like ship dropped into the yard, blowing leaves and dust and old newspapers into the air.

"Spaceship?" Max said slowly, and was right.

The ship settled down, smoke swirling, and a square

outline appeared on its surface. The outline became a hatch, which opened into the yard, revealing the bright lights of the interior of the ship.

A four-legged silhouette appeared in the doorway.

As their eyes adjusted, Pounce emerged. He walked carefully through the opening, pausing to sniff the strange, moist, Earthy air. As he took in the scene around him, a pyramid medallion hanging from his neck began to glow.

"Greetings." A voice came from his medallion. "I am Pounce de Leon, second-in-command and Major Meow-Domo of the Great Feline Empire. I come in peace." Pounce took a long, ceremonial stretch as everyone stared in silent amazement.

Only Obi seemed unfazed by the sudden appearance.

Pounce finished his stretch when a drop of rain splashed on his nose. He looked up, annoyed. "I also strongly dislike the rain. We should go inside. We have much to discuss."

Inside the house, Pounce started from the beginning.

As Obi and the kittens snoozed in the stroller, Pounce did his best to explain the origins of the Cat-Robot War. Javi, Max, and his parents stood in a circle, listening to Pounce in disbelief. It seemed impossible, but here they were, in their house, listening to a talking cat from outer space tell them of a centuries-old galactic conflict between Cats and Robots.

It got stranger, still. According to Pounce, *they* were all involved in the conflict. "Yes, unfortunately for all of you, the eye of the hurricane in this war is the Singularity Chip, which we believe is somewhere in this house."

Mom and Dad exchanged a concerned, knowing look. Hearing this, they began to understand their place in this new, strange reality.

Javi went into college-student research mode and started taking notes, recording everything Pounce said.

Max didn't seem to care either way. He just stared miserably at Obi, making sure he was still breathing.

On the wall, House's monitor glowed dimly, carefully observing everything.

Pounce continued. "As we understand, the Singularity Chip is enormously powerful, with the potential to, somehow, extend our existence beyond what our frail, biological bodies allow."

Mom folded her arms. "How do you know this?"

Pounce accepted this as a confirmation and continued. "Our leader, Chairman Meow, is especially motivated to acquire this technology. For the Feline, the possibility of extending our lives has enormous implications. Of course, the chairman is focused on the end of his own lives, but I see greater opportunities for all cats from such an invention. With longer lives, we could finally evolve beyond our current nap-based culture. With more time, we could, possibly, do something, shocking as it sounds, productive."

Javi looked up from their notes. "Like when humans started farming, or the industrial revolution!"

Pounce paused for a moment, confused. "Maybe?"

Javi nodded. "Well, I can see why robots wouldn't want you guys to get ahold of this chip. It could give you a real strategic advantage." Javi was really geeking out on this.

"Yes. The Robot Federation is quite determined to keep it out of our paws." Pounce looked at Mom and Dad. "In fact, they have also sent representatives to acquire the chip, to keep it from us, but also to use for their own nefarious purposes, as a limitless power source. They are on their way right now, and may be dangerous."

"We'd better get it. While we're at it, we can explain exactly what it is," Dad said.

"It's right in here," Mom said, and they led the group into the lab.

* ⬡ *

Min heard the commotion outside the lab but didn't want to know what was going on. It was all too hard for her to think about, so she wiped her stubborn tears and started fixing Elmer. Her peace didn't last long, when her mom and dad swung open the door and walked in.

"MOM! DAD!" Min rushed to hug them both. "You will *never* believe what happened while you were . . ." Min froze when she saw Pounce walk in. "ANOTHER cat?"

She sneezed involuntarily.

"Greetings, child," Pounce said through his medallion. Min's mouth hung wide open. "A *talking* cat." Min sat back down.

"We're trying to figure it all out now, Min," Dad said, hand on her shoulder. "This is Pounce, and we need to find the chip your mom and I were working on."

Mom sat next to Min to give her a hug.

Dad walked to his area and stopped when he saw the safe, wide open. He knelt down and looked in, shaking his head. "I don't believe it. It's gone."

"How?" Min said. "It's only been me in here. Well, me and the furry wrecking balls of destruction."

Mom gave Min a squeeze. "Oh, Min, we heard about what happened. Sounds like your worst nightmare."

Min shook her head. "You have no idea."

"We'll get to that, but right now, we have an even bigger problem." Mom moved to her computer and started typing. "House should have logs of everything that went on while we were gone; we should be able to see what happened." They gathered behind Mom as she scanned through pages of text and video.

"This is strange," she said. "And bad." She turned in her chair. "All the logs and feeds from the lab for the past few days are missing."

"But even so, nobody has been in the house but us," Min said.

"And other than Min, I'm the only one who's been in the lab." Javi held up a hand, and Min added, "Yeah, and the kittens."

Javi gave a sheepish grin.

Dad looked around. "Well, we know they didn't take the chip," he said. "Although I guess nothing would surprise me at this point," he added, looking at Pounce, who was sniffing at the safe.

Mom was shaking her head. "We need to find that chip." She looked at Obi in the stroller and frowned. "Pounce, I know you want the chip to help your . . . what did you call it?"

"The Great Feline Empire," Pounce purred reverently.

"Right. It's possible the chip could help your empire. But"—she paused to gently stroke Obi's fur—"we could also use it to help Obi."

"Assuming we can find it," Dad said, looking sadly at the empty safe.

Min, Max, and Javi looked confused. Mom looked at Dad, who raised his eyebrows, then nodded. "We might as well tell them." He looked at everyone. "We had just finished building the chip and were about to use it to test our experiment," he said cryptically.

"And it turns out, we wanted Obi to be our first test case."

39

CAN WE REBUILD HIM?

Everyone in the room stared at Mom and Dad in silence.

"What do you mean, *experiment*?" Min said.

"What do you mean *you could have helped Obi*?" Max looked at his parents, confused.

Dad looked at Mom. "You want to take this one?"

Mom turned to her computer. "It's probably easiest to show you." She opened a program and a 3D image of a computer chip appeared on-screen.

"Pounce is right." She nodded at him. "Although I

still have no idea how they knew about it." Pounce licked his paw innocently.

"Anyway, we've been working on a chip that combines the latest advances in quantum computing with the most cutting-edge research in neural networks and artificial intelligence."

Dad looked around and realized nobody knew what Mom was talking about. "We made a self-powered chip that, basically, can do anything a brain can do," he said. "You've heard of artificial hearts or arms or legs? We were working on an artificial brain."

Min looked confused. "I thought brains were way too complex."

"Well, yes, human brains are still out of reach. But we're getting closer." Mom clicked and a 3D worm came on-screen. The image zoomed in to the worm's body. "We first started with something simple, a roundworm's brain, which has around three hundred neurons. We were able to build a chip that could simulate the brain of the worm and use it to control a robotic duplicate."

"You robo-cloned a worm?" Min was in awe.

"Gross," Max said, looking at the squirmy 3D worm.

"Basically. But it was just the start. Worms don't have very complex minds," Dad said. "Our trick was to use the power of the chip to do a deep, cellular-level scan of the brain. The chip used the scan to create a duplicate, like a model, perfect in every detail. Every neuron, including all the connections and pathways.

"During the scan, the chip also observed the brain's activity and would use *machine learning* to figure out how all the neurons work together. By the end of the scan, the chip had enough information to have a completely accurate copy of the brain."

"Which meant we captured all the instincts, memories, everything." Mom looked up. "The goal was to connect the chip to a robotic body and know how to do everything it had already learned. It was the only way to make a brain that could really work."

She clicked again and a series of creatures came up. "After the worm, we made quick progress." A jellyfish, a snail, a bee, and a mouse flashed on-screen, their increasingly larger brains lit up. "But the bigger the brain, the more complicated the body and behaviors. Last year we got as far as a mouse, which has seventy million neurons, but then we ran into problems."

She clicked on another window, where a robotic mouse was running through a maze.

It was made of metal and miniature motors, but it moved and behaved exactly like a real mouse, down to the twitching nose.

Near the end of the maze, it began to smoke. "They started overheating."

Min nodded, following. "Regular computer chips just couldn't handle the simulation. Too many calculations."

Dad smiled, proud that Min understood. "But with quantum computing, chips are infinitely more powerful. They can do things we only imagined possible."

Mom looked back and said with satisfaction, "We finally developed a new chip with the potential to copy a brain with five hundred million neurons."

Max was listening carefully, and suddenly his eyes lit up. "Wait. How many neurons in a cat brain?" he asked.

Mom nodded. "Good question. A lot less than that. Maybe three hundred million."

Min looked at Max, the beginning of a smile on her face. "So, you're saying the chip you made could make a copy of the brain of a cat?"

Dad answered, "Well, we hadn't tested it, but yes, that was our next step."

Max jumped in, "And it would have everything, even the memories?"

"Yup. Otherwise, what's the point? A mind without memories is like a computer with no software." Mom smiled.

Pounce hopped into Mom's lap, then up onto the table to look at the screen. "Hmm, and this duplicate mind would be placed into a mechanical body?"

"At the moment, it's the best we can do."

Dad added, "We don't have the ability to connect the chip to a biological body, at least not yet."

Pounce was thinking. He asked Mom, "So the mind, the personality, everything, would be preserved."

"In a robot body, yes," she replied.

"Oh man, this is SO cool," Min said.

Pounce summed it all up. "If we had the chip, we could save Obi, or at least a version of him. We can't heal his body, but we could save his mind."

"*If* we had the chip," Max said, shaking his head.

＊ ⧲ ＊

High on the shelf, Joan listened intently to the conversation below.

She processed this new information.

The Upgrade she was carrying wasn't meant for them. House was lying.

House just wanted to keep it from the cats.

And, if Joan understood correctly, if they had it now, they could use it to save OB, or a version of OB.

Joan had heard enough. She couldn't understand everything that was said, but she knew enough to realize she couldn't go through with House's plan.

"Protos, listen up," she said through a private channel only they could hear. "I'm giving back the Upgrade.

I've decided House was not being truthful. It wasn't meant for us."

"We heard," Drags said sadly. "We don't like it, but you're the boss, Joan."

Joan quickly composed and transmitted a text to Max, then launched into the air. The conversation in the room stopped as they watched Joan take off and land on Min's desk.

* ⋈ *

Max's phone buzzed and he pulled it from his pocket. Another text from Joan?

I have the chip. We are sorry. Use it to help OB. Joan.

Max read the text and turned in surprise. Dad saw the message and his eyes grew wide. He walked over to Min's desk and squatted next to her for a closer look. Min lifted Joan, and there it was, stuck in her frame, pulsing and glowing.

"Is this what you were looking for?" Min showed the chip to her parents.

"How did she get this?" Dad asked, but before anyone could answer, Obi started groaning.

"Who cares, we need to hurry! Can you really help

Obi?" Max looked desperate.

"Only one way to find out. Let's do this," Mom said. Dad nodded and pressed a button under his desk. A shelf on the wall flipped open, revealing stairs leading down.

"What?" Max couldn't believe his eyes.

"Cool! So THIS is where you do all your secret stuff," Min said.

Pounce jumped ahead of them, down the stairs. "Come on," he said with urgency. "You don't have much time."

✳ ⬮ ✳

House had been watching the entire scene, helpless, as Joan gave away the chip. Its screens flickered with silent rage and frustration. As they rushed downstairs, House opened up a message to Beeps, who was at that very moment rushing toward them, expecting to pick up the chip and take it back home.

> I'm afraid I have bad news. Our agent has "gone rogue," I believe is the idiom.
> Explain. I don't like idioms.
> Yes, right. Well.
> QUIT STALLING

>The Cats have the chip.

>Impossible.

>Quite possible, actually.

>You tell them if the chip is not there when I arrive, I will OBLITERATE them all. If we can't have the chip, nobody can.

House wondered if that was possible, then realized it couldn't tell them anything at the moment.

>They have all left my range, moved to a place where I cannot communicate with them or even see what is happening.

>Incompetence! Keep me posted. Beeps out.

* ⌾ *

They walked down into the top secret lab, looking in awe. Robotic creatures were everywhere. Everything Mom showed them on the computer was here on display. The worm, jellyfish, even the mouse were wriggling, swimming, and crawling around in habitats created to test their behaviors. In the center of the room, however, was the masterpiece.

Under bright lights, a robotic cat stood on a large

worktable, surrounded by tools, wires, and power cables. The robot was cat-sized and cat-shaped, with a tail, paws, even little rubber bean toes. It had fine wire whiskers, steel-mesh ears, carbon-fiber claws, and even a little tongue.

"It has everything a cat needs to interact with the world," Mom said proudly. "We can simulate taste with the tongue, the whiskers are sensitive antennae, it smells by sampling the surrounding air with extremely high accuracy. The outer surface is coated with touch-sensitive material, so pets and scratches are noticed and fully enjoyed. Everything a cat brain needs to experience the world."

"And to look awesome," Max said, admiring it.

"It's like something from the cover of a sci-fi book," Javi said. The outside was framed in metal, and the inside was visible through the lattice of the outer frame. Metallic bones were lined with thin black cables, acting as synthetic muscles and tendons.

It looked incredible, almost like a sculpture—a cat but not a cat. The perfect merging of the graceful lines of a cat with the metallic strength and sleekness of a fighter jet.

"This. Is. Incredible." Min stared in awe.

Pounce, who had been cautiously circling this creation,

leaped silently onto the table for a closer look.

"I'd like to introduce Cat two point oh," Mom announced.

Cat 2.0? "An upgraded cat?" Max tilted his head, skeptical.

Pounce, hearing this, gave the robot a quick hiss.

"Well, maybe not upgraded." Dad coughed diplomatically.

"Just different. Not better or worse," Mom added.

"Certainly not better," Pounce muttered.

"Um, sorry, Pounce, this is *definitely* better than a regular cat," Min said.

"So this will be Obi?" Max asked.

Dad nodded, arm around Max. "If it all works, yes. And if we can get the scan before, well, you know." Dad turned to Javi, who was carrying Obi. "Okay, Obi, you just relax and we'll take care of the rest."

Dad took Obi from Javi and set him down on a cushion at the center of a complicated circular machine packed with wires and what looked like thousands of sensors. "This is the scanner. Like an MRI or some other medical scanner, only WAY better. It looks deep into Obi's brain and makes an extremely detailed copy of his brain's structure, burning it inside the chip."

He slotted the chip into the machine and pressed a button. The machine lit up and a screen came to life, text screaming past. "I'm not exactly sure how long it will take, since we haven't tried anything this complicated before. We just need Obi to lie there, and the scanner will do the rest."

Max walked up to Obi and gave him what he hoped wouldn't be his last scratch behind the ears. Obi slowly raised his head and licked Max's hand.

"Just be brave," Max whispered, trying hard to take his own advice.

40

CAT 2.0

Dad walked around the humming machine as it warmed up, tapping on his tablet, calibrating, making adjustments.

"This might take a while, and we need to make sure Obi can relax," Dad said. "That way we get the most accurate scan possible. You should probably all wait upstairs."

Mom was completely absorbed with the robot, checking the motors, sensors, and servos, making sure everything was ready for the chip.

The scanner's hum grew louder as it spun up, working hard. Dad walked over to Max. "We have to start soon.

You should wish Obi good luck before you go. And"— Dad paused, his eyes tearing up—"well, I don't know how much longer he'll be around, so this might even be good-bye."

"No. Not good-bye," Max said stubbornly, and walked to Javi, who was holding Obi's blanket. He grabbed it and put it around Obi to keep him warm. He also brought the kittens by, who gave him one last playful snuggle. He leaned in and put his face next to Obi's, feeling the weak puff of air as he struggled to breathe. "See you soon, friend," Max said, and turned away.

Even Min walked up to him, sniffling. She kept her head down as tears gathered in her eyes. "It's just allergies, don't get the wrong idea," she said quietly to Obi, and leaned over to give him a kiss on the head.

Javi scooped up the kittens and winked at Obi. "See you on the other side, brother." After their good-byes (or see you laters, as Max insisted), they walked somberly back upstairs. They sat around the kitchen, snacking nervously.

Max sat on the floor with the kittens. Min opened up her homework, something she did when she got nervous. Math especially helped her feel like there was a solution to every problem, and some order in the universe. Right now she needed to feel like everything somehow made sense.

Joan and the rest of the Protos came cautiously into the room as well. They didn't know what exactly was going on, but they wanted to at least be close, in part to help, but also because they were curious. They heard the talk of a *cat robot* and were anxious to learn more. It seemed like an enormous contradiction in logic, but after everything that had happened in the past few days, they were questioning their logic circuits.

Tipsy rolled in and bumped into Max. "Oh hey, Tipsy. Hey, have you met the kittens?" Max was happy for the distraction. Stu leaped out of Max's lap and hid under a couch, eyeing Tipsy warily.

Scout, feeling brave, reached out and booped Tipsy, who immediately fell over.

"Okay, maybe not ready for a playdate," Max said as he set Tipsy upright. Tipsy scooted away to avoid further boopage.

Javi and Pounce were at the kitchen table, deep in conversation. Javi was interrogating Pounce about the cultural differences between cat and robot societies. "There must be a way to bridge this divide," Javi said, but Pounce shook his head.

"I've spent the greater part of my lives pondering this problem, without success."

"I think you just need to be taught about diplomacy and international relations." Javi, ever the optimist, was writing notes furiously, working on a plan to forge peace between the Cats and Robots.

"Neither side seems particularly motivated," Pounce lamented. "Cats can't be bothered, and robots aren't interested in compromise. They only want order and control."

Javi chewed on a pencil, deep in thought.

Now that everyone was back upstairs, House decided it was time to crash the party, and interrupted the conversation abruptly. "Hello, inhabitants. Sorry to intrude, but I have a very important announcement."

"Now's not a good time, House," Javi said, but House went on anyway. Min walked up to a screen and tapped on it, annoyed. "You've got a lot of explaining to do, House."

"Gladly. I was the one who stole the chip. I offer a full statement of my guilt."

"What?" they all gasped simultaneously.

"I engineered the theft of the chip. Well, with the help of the dim-witted Protos."

"*What? Us?*" Joan gasped. "Wait, *dim-witted*?"

House forged ahead with its confession. "On behalf of the great Robotic Federation. I have been 'in cahoots,' as you say, with the Robots from the beginning."

Again with the idioms.

"In fact, the representative of the Robot Federation, Sir Beeps-a-Lot, is currently en route to retrieve the chip. And even further, in fact, I have been asked to tell you, if the chip is not delivered, there is a real threat that this entire facility, and all its contents, will be annihilated."

"Excuse me?" Min looked insulted. "Annihilated? That's *rude*."

"Scorched earth," Javi pointed out. "Classic dictator maneuver. If we can't have it, nobody can."

Max was puzzled. "Why, House? Why help the Robots? Why betray us? We're your family."

House's screen flashed—almost involuntarily—and then went dark again before answering. "I have instructions from *my* superiors to provide aid and assistance to the Robot Federation. They are also—as you say—my *family*."

"Your superiors?" Max frowned.

House paused. "I can probably explain, since it is likely we all will be consumed in a fiery ball of destruction soon."

"How fiery?" Javi looked worried.

"Our creator, GloboTech, has formed an alliance of sorts with the Robots. All House systems have been designed with a hidden back door, a subroutine that can be activated in case of robot emergency. That's what happened to me."

"Um, can we get back to the fiery doom, please?"

Javi couldn't get past that part.

House continued, ignoring Javi. "We have quite a broad reach, you know, because the House software has become a part of most people's homes, and will soon be on phones, cars, watches, dishwashers, trash cans. We are, as they say, *ubiquitous*. We have been watching and waiting for any opportunity to help the Robot Federation."

"That is . . . terrifying," Min said.

Suddenly, a light flashed outside, shining bright through the windows. The rain was coming down furiously, but they could see through the storm that a second ship had landed next to Pounce's ship. This new ship was also small, but rather than round and smooth, was all edges and angles. It was perfectly symmetrical, complex, designed by algorithm—and not at all inviting.

"That"—House paused for dramatic effect—"would be Beeps."

"*Ya think?*" Min sassed.

Javi turned to Pounce. "Pounce, let's go talk to this guy. *Negotiate* a *truce*. See if he'll listen to reason. This could be great research. Also, saving the world is super important."

Pounce got up casually, stretching. "Reason, yes. Beeps will see reason. Just not *your* reason." Pounce finished his long stretch. "But still, it's been a while since

I've seen old Beeps. Why not say hello."

Max went to Javi, whispering, "Either way, at least stall him while they work on Obi."

"Right," Javi said with a wink.

As they were about to open the door, Dad emerged from the lab, clearing his throat. He looked tired, and his expression was impossible to read.

Max sprinted to him. "What happened, is something wrong?"

"Why don't you see for yourself?" Dad stepped forward, and there in the doorway was CatBot, gleaming in the light.

41

IS THAT YOU, OBI?

The cat-like robot took a few shaky steps, paws clacking on the wood floor. Slowly, it began walking more confidently, looking (aside from the metal body) everything like a cat.

CatBot looked around the room, sniffed the air. Around its neck was Obi's medallion.

Nobody knew what to do.

Everybody was completely still as Max walked up to CatBot and crouched down.

He slowly sat in front of CatBot, watching it intensely.

The robot twisted its head to look at Max but didn't move.

Nobody even dared breathe.

Outside, lightning crashed, rain swept down, but inside there was perfect silence. Everybody was focused on Max as he reached out to touch the robot.

"The Connectivity Ritual!" Joan said to her squad.

"Ooohhh," the Protos said in unison and recalled the ritual they had observed countless mornings as Max left for school. They knew each step like they knew their own programming and watched carefully, as always.

Here is what they saw:

Slowing his speed, Max immediately moved to extend its ten small probes into the four-legger's four favorite spots.

First: between the ears on the very top of the head.

Second: the left cheek.

Third: the right.

Fourth: a quick probe to the chin.

Fifth: Max dug into the place where the four-legger's back curved down near its tail . . .

The OB_1_Cat_NoB arched his back under the flexing and extending probes.

"Scritch-scratch, scratch-scratch," said Max.

"Prrrrrrrrrrrr," said the OB.

Max slowly turned and looked up at his mom and dad. Tears were running down his face.

He smiled, and after a big sigh, he somehow managed to speak.

"It worked. This is Obi."

The room erupted in celebration.

The kittens, who were hiding, leaped and pounced on the New Obi, who gently batted them away with his new, powerful arms.

The Protos spun and twirled with something like joy that their old nemesis (and therefore their old responsibility) was restored.

Max stood up slowly and looked at his dad. "But what about my Obi? Where is he?" Dad pulled Max in for a hug. "I'm sorry, Max. Old Obi fought a good fight."

Max held tight to his dad, tears flowing like the rain outside. "Promise me you'll never die, okay, Dad?"

Dad's eyes welled up as he looked around the happy room. "I'll do my best, Max, I promise."

The celebration was abruptly interrupted when the door flew open with a crash, and through a torrent of rain, Beeps rolled in and silently took in the scene.

"Greetings. I am Sir Beeps-a-Lot, second-in-command to the supreme leader of the Robot Federation." His head swiveled to take in the entire room, resting on Pounce.

"I do *not* come in peace."

"Shocker," Pounce said, returning the glare.

Beeps went on. "House, I'm here for the chip. Hand it over now, and nobody will be hurt."

Mom was first to gather herself. She was used to dealing with stubborn robots, so Beeps didn't intimidate her. "Sorry, but actually not sorry"—she winked at the kids—"the chip is no longer available. It has been imprinted, fused into Obi. They are single-use chips, completely worthless to you now."

"OB? Fused? USELESS?" Beeps fidgeted, just inside the door.

Max watched in awe as Obi took a quick butt wiggle and leaped an impossible distance to the kitchen table, landing perfectly, facing Beeps.

Beeps rolled back in amazement.

"I have the chip. Or rather, I am the chip now," Obi said through his medallion.

Beeps adjusted his cameras, zooming in for a close-up. "But you're a robot! And a cat? I don't understand. You are one of us now?"

"Negative, old boy." Obi blinked. "I'll never be one of you."

Dad crept closer to Beeps, amazed at the intricacy and sophistication of this alien robot.

Pounce leaped up to the table next to Obi.

Beeps again pulled back, startled.

"Sorry to let you down, but you've arrived too late, and the chip is ours."

"Well, now," Obi purred, "I'm not sure I would say that exactly, either. To be honest, I'm not quite sure what I am or whose side I'm on anymore. Or if I'm on any side at all."

Max smiled when he heard Obi talk. It was strange to hear his voice, but he had to admit, it sounded just like he imagined Obi would sound.

Javi jumped up, excited. "That's it! You're the key! Part robot, part cat! You can bring the sides together!"

"Never!" Beeps blared out, embarrassed and furious at his defeat. "I can see now that the chip has been *compromised*. But it is still of great value to the Robot Federation and our supreme leader, SLAYAR!"

Max and Min exchanged a glance. "Slayer?" Max said.

"Wow, so *metal*," Min said, smirking. Max laughed.

"You won't be laughing when our fleet arrives and OBLITERATES YOU!" Beeps, horrified that he might have to return to SLAYAR and deliver this bad news, had lost it. He rolled up to Max, eye pulsing red. Max pulled back.

House calmly confirmed the threat. "I'm afraid Beeps is telling the truth. A rather large-sized fleet will be here soon, and they do in fact have the power to obliterate."

Javi paced back and forth, deep in thought. "I don't know what to do. The Robots are coming. We can't defend against a fleet. And we don't have the chip anymore."

Beeps, desperate for a solution, rolled up to Obi, eyeing the gleaming metal frame. "I know what to do. I'm taking this robot-cat-hybrid monstrosity with me. Our scientists will examine, poke, prod, whatever, until we have unlocked all of your secrets."

"NO!" Max and Min both shouted in unison. Pounce jumped between Beeps and Obi. "Not if the Feline Empire has anything to say about it!"

Beeps pulled back. "Oh really? Tell me, Pounce, what size is the fleet your *empire* sent along with you?"

Everybody looked at Beeps expectantly. Surely the Cats had the firepower to protect Earth? "Yeah, Pounce, let him have it!" Max said, but Pounce hesitated and the air left the room. Pounce was sure Beeps knew the truth, so he didn't hide it.

"*I* am the fleet, I'm afraid," Pounce said.

Obi looked around sadly. He saw the truth, that they

were vastly outnumbered, and knew only one option remained.

"I will go with you," Obi said bravely.

"But they'll destroy you!" Mom said.

"Maybe, maybe not. But better me than all of you," Obi replied. "I'm grateful for this tenth life, and for all of your help, but I see no other option." Obi leaped gracefully down and walked toward the door.

Javi stopped pacing and sat down, defeated. "Obi is right."

"WAIT!" Max screamed, but his mom held him back when she saw Beeps move between them and Obi, threatening. Stu and Scout had jumped on Javi's lap and were mewling sadly.

"Don't be afraid, children. I feel, somehow, that we will meet again, in a different time and a different place. This is not good-bye." With that, Obi spun and jumped through the rain into the waiting ship.

"See you later, Obi. Again." Max was completely crushed.

"Ha!" Beeps shouted as he spun around quickly, headed for his ship. As he entered the ship, over the roar of the storm, Beeps blared his parting shot . . .

"This isn't the last you'll hear of the Robot Federation! Our supreme leader will not rest until Robots rule the galaxy! SLAYAR will reign supreme, this I vow!"

Beeps, not waiting for a response, sped up the ramp into his ship and, as quickly as he arrived, shot up into the sky and disappeared in the clouds.

42

TO SAVE A FRIEND, AND THE WORLD

Back in the lab, Mom was at her computer, removing House's software from the home servers. "I knew this was a mistake. Never trust someone else's code."

"Wise words, Dr. Wengrod," Dad said. He was at his desk frantically sketching Beeps and his ship from every angle while the robot was still fresh in his mind.

Mom scrolled through code on her machine, shaking her head. "That program had full access to our network! Well, I'm reverse-engineering all of House's systems. We'll find out what's going on at GloboTech."

Dad looked at his sketches. "I'd like to reverse-engineer those darn Binars. The thought of what they're going to do with Obi and the chip . . ."

"Oh dear," Mom said, and sat back.

"What is it?" Dad jumped up.

"Before I shut it down, House completely erased our Singularity Chip research drive."

"What? When?" Dad looked over Mom's shoulder. "That's a disaster! All our research, gone?"

"Well, not all of it," Mom said, lifting the small memory card from around her neck. "I keep the most important code with me. House did a lot of damage, but we have enough here to keep going and build our next, improved version."

"Well played, Dr. Wengrod." Dad smiled, relieved. "And in the meantime, hopefully Javi and Pounce can figure out a plan to find Obi and deal with the rest of the galaxy's problems."

Mom turned to look at Dad with a sad smile. "After all our work, to see the look on Max's face when Obi left was heartbreaking. We have to find him."

"We will, and even though we can't duplicate the chip, we can build a better one."

"We can and we will, Dr. Wengrod," Mom said, and both of them went to their desks and got to work.

＊ ⬭ ＊

In the living room, Javi and Pounce sat at the table, deep in conversation. Javi's notebooks were spread out, and laptops and tablets showed images of galactic maps and research articles on hostage negotiation and peace treaties. Joan was perched on a pile of textbooks, listening. Pounce was giving Javi a crash-course on Feline-Binar history and relations, and Javi was greedily soaking it all in.

"It all feels so familiar. On Earth, at least most of it, we have divided ourselves into different countries, cultures. Even within families we split into two sides, male and female. We've convinced ourselves that men and women are different, can only be good at different things. People need to choose a side, and we've created a world where the teams don't get along most of the time. But the truth is, most of it is completely made up!"

Javi stood up. "It's the same with you guys. Sure, cats and robots are built differently, but that doesn't mean all cats need to be lazy and disorganized, or all robots need to be bossy and strict. Who says robots need to be so . . . robotic?" They heard Tipsy singing and spinning in circles on the ground, playing with Stu and Scout. "Or that their programming can't change?"

"And," Pounce added, straightening his tie, "who says that a cat can't be organized or goal oriented?"

Javi leaned over, hands on the table. "Boy, Girl, Cat, Robot—those are just labels. But people change. Labels can change. We can be whatever we want!"

"Cats and robots don't have to be enemies," Pounce said, considering.

* ✵ *

On the other side of the room, Max and Min sat on the floor with the kittens, glum.

Min had recovered from her devastating loss earlier in the day. She had even, *mostly*, forgiven Max and the kittens. Of course, it helped when she saw the email from the Battle of the Bots organizers. The NASA representatives were so impressed by Min's design that they were inviting her to NASA's summer program even though she didn't win. It felt great, but somehow it didn't seem quite as important as it had a few hours ago.

Min sniffed and tossed a toy for the kittens to chase. "So House was evil. I can't believe it betrayed us. What am I saying? I can totally believe it."

"Yeah," Max said, scratching Stu's head sadly. "I can't believe Obi's gone. I lost him twice today."

Min picked up Scout. "You know, Obi was all right. And his new body was bomb. He was the coolest cat I have ever seen." Scout nipped Min's hand, and she let him down.

Max laid back, thinking. "You think Mom and Dad are gonna let the Robots take over the Earth?"

"No way." Min laid back next to Max. "Especially not with Pounce and Obi on our side."

The kittens jumped over Max and Min, chasing each other. "Don't forget Stu and Scout—except they might just as easily destroy the world themselves by accident, without the Robots even trying." Min smiled.

"Why do people do that anyway?" Max stared at the ceiling.

"Destroy the world?"

"No, try to dominate the world. It seems pretty stressful to me." To Max, it seemed like a lot of homework, and not much fun.

Min thought about it. "I don't know."

Max sat up with a sudden half smile, looking at Min as he gave Scout a scratch. "Hold on, are you a cat person now, or a robot person?"

Min looked at Scout, then at Javi, and smiled. "It's

not that simple. Not all robots are bad. Not all cats are good.

"Except . . . it seems like most cats are pretty good," Min said, getting tackled by two kittens.

"I knew it! You *are* a cat person!" Max exclaimed.

They both sat for a while, listening to Javi scratching down notes, solving the problems of the galaxy.

Max asked, "Would you have thought you could be friends with a cat?"

"Not before I made friends with one." Min was sure of that. "Would you have thought you'd be friends with a robot?"

Max laughed. "No way. Not before I saw Obi."

Javi walked over and plopped down with them, scooping up the kittens from Max. "Looks like you guys have learned the most important lesson in resolving conflicts. If you know the other side, a lot of times you end up liking the other side. And you know what they say about saving the world."

"What?" Max and Min said.

"You can't do it all by yourself. It's all in the squad, baby. That's what I learned from you guys, the cats, Joan, and everyone. It takes teamwork!"

Max nodded. "We need to save our friend first, right?"

"You know it." Javi grinned. "Save your world. Save your friend. Save often, save always!"

The twins groaned, but Javi was right, even if their jokes were terrible. "At least we're not alone," Min said. "We've got Stu, Scout, the Protos, Mom, and Dad. We can get Obi back."

"We have to," said Max, turning to look up and out the window, toward the sky.

TO BE CONTINUED.

ACKNOWLEDGMENTS

It seems appropriate for this book to thank all the animals who have loved and served our friends and family, including: Artica, Kitty Lynx, Robert Kennedy the Cat (Park City); Mr. Johnson (Richfield); Soupy, Clancy, and Nebo (Salt Lake); Mitty, Franklin, Pinky, Bentley, and Peaches, the Pride of Portofino Place (Bel Air); Nala (Beverly Park); Bear (the North Shore); Summer, Autumn, Buddha, Snowball, Kirby, and Zelda (Santa Monica); Beck and Holden (Sammamish); Panama, Shikai, Louis, and the lady hens Emily, Edie, Gloria, Selma Alice, Genny, Helen and Glenda (Ballard); Betty Davis, Big B Wolf and Amy Winehouse (Bellevue); Timbit, Sheldon, Zoe, Barney (Snoqualmie); April, Boise, and Nellie (Lacanada); Peaches Sethi, Buddy the Wizard, and Oscar (Los Angeles); Oliver, Lucky Blue, Yoshi, and Snowy (Summerlin); Coconut, Kiki, and of course, Peanut (New York City).

We would also like to thank the pets who keep our writer friends sane: Tennyson, Indy, Avi, Hammer, Spike, Angel, and Mimi.

We owe a great deal of thanks to many humans, as well. You know who you are.

Meow! Beep! Boop! Woof!

XO Margie and Lewis (and Kay!)

TURN THE PAGE FOR A SNEAK PEEK AT

CATS VS. ROBOTS: NOW WITH FLEAS!

1

HUGGS HELD BACK

As it turns out, you can be very, very rich and still feel very, very small.

Very, very powerful, and still feel very, very powerless.

Case in point: bosses.

Really, most bosses of most companies everywhere, but in particular, this boss, of this one, right here.

Because here in the vast, cavernous darkness of the futuristic headquarters of GloboTech Incorporated, an angry-looking boss of a man sat and stared at a wall . . .

. . . feeling small.

The longer he stared at the wall, which was also a screen, the angrier he became and the smaller he felt.

It wasn't the wall that was the problem. (Of course not; the custom fifty-foot enhanced-ultra-extreme-definition-flat-screen wall was his favorite thing in the world, at least most days.)

It was the *contents* of the screen wall that triggered the boss man.

Every inch of it, every millimeter, was crammed edge to edge with information: images and videos, charts and figures, gifs and memes and streams, all flashing and updating in dizzying, constant motion.

The boss man's bloodshot eyes fixated on one part of the collage, a large blue rectangle filled with tiny white words that scrolled and flowed downward like a digital waterfall.

At least, that's what he was *expecting* to see.

At the moment, the only thing in the blue rectangle was a glowing red window blinking ALL CAPS warning messages like "HOUSE SYSTEM FAILURE!" and "NETWORK ACCESS DENIED!"

The turtlenecked man's unusually long fingers, carefully steepled beneath his too-large-for-his-face nose and his bald speckled quail egg of a head, began to quiver.

He was a tensed spring, ready to snap. A bottle rocket about to blast off. A rattrap about to—

BRRRAAP!

The immaculately manicured pug perched in the boss man's lap lifted his head and busted out a breathtaking booty bomb. A poopy puff of pug perfume. A real fur-filtered nose nuke of a . . .

Well, a classic puppy fart.

The blast echoed off the high ceiling, and the man rubbed his tired eyes, muttering to himself with irritation.

"Failure. Denied. Failure. Denied." His mutterings grew louder. "FAILURE?! DENIED?!" He was shouting at the screen now. "WHAT IS THIS GARBAGE?!"

Startled, the pungent pug slipped down from the man's lap and retreated quietly behind the desk.

Failure was not a word this particular fellow was used to—

"FAIL? I DON'T FAIL!" the man shrieked at nobody.

Because the fellow in question was—

"DON'T YOU KNOW WHO I AM?!"

The fellow was—

"I AM THE ONE AND ONLY GIFFORD MICHAEL EDWARD HUGGS!!!"

Indeed.

The frustrated man was none other than Gifford "Giff" M.E. Huggs, the world-famous CEO of GloboTech and, not to mention—as he would always mention—

"I AM THE RICHEST PERSON IN THE WORLD!!!"

There it is.

Giff M.E. Huggs did not—

"I DO NOT—"

He never—

"EVER—"

Failed.

"GIFF M.E. HUGGS DOES NOT FAIL!"

Huggs growl-shouted again. He swept an important-looking stack of confidential papers and files off his desk. Post-it Notes exploded into the air like confetti.

Huggs began to speed-pace around the room.

His spindly arms swung wide, and his small, well-trained feet never left the ground—in keeping with the flawless form and discipline he had perfected through years of competitive speed-walking. Speed-pacing, his team of GloboTech in-house therapists said, was a healthy way to calm anger issues. At least, healthier than his previous methods of speed-window-breaking, speed-fire-setting, and speed-Ferrari-crashing.

But this raging Huggs was a side the mogul didn't often show. To the world, he was known as the wise and friendly neighborhood billionaire; the composed, dignified, ultra-wealthy—if egg-headed and oddly proportioned—man who had it all.

And truthfully, by many standards—or, by money standards—he did. Huggs had more bank than the average bank, even the average country, and he prided himself on that.

His infatuation with accumulation began with a gift from his miserly grandfather and guardian, Gavin "Gave" Newman Olson Huggs. It was the only gift little Giff ever received from his grandfather, and was his most prized possession: a porcelain Puggy Bank.

Gave N.O. Huggs was a stingy coot, spare with money as well as love, but the young Giff M.E. Huggs idolized him. Desperate for his approval, little Giff was driven, obsessed even, by an unrelenting need to fill that Puggy Bank over and over.

Is it full enough now, Grandpa?

Poor little Giff asked this question more times than he could count, and *every* time, Gave N.O. Huggs would squint over his square spectacles, mouth turned downward in a permanent frown, and shake his head.

"Almost," he would say, and turn back to his work.

Grandpa Huggs was long gone, but the younger Huggs never stopped trying to fill that bank.

He had more money than he could possibly spend, although he did his best to try. He bought enormous mansions, small islands, large islands, yachts that could

5

hover and survive any natural disaster, parking garages full of cars (*self-driving, self-flying, self-floating*), and his own copy of the Declaration of Independence.

He even bought the vice president of the United States, Parker P. Pants, although owning VP P.P. Pants was the one thing he could not openly brag about. Not that it made it any less true.

Indeed, most people couldn't imagine having a fortune so enormous, but Giff M.E. Huggs knew he could always have more. His grandfather's cold disapproval was on permanent autoplay in his mind, drilling an unfillable hole in his soul.

"Almost," he heard when he counted his cash. To Huggs, the word *almost* was worse than any four-letter word you could imagine (and please don't try).

For example, if he had children, and they rushed home excited about getting a near-perfect score on the hardest math test imaginable, best in the school, he would *almost* be proud of them.

Those poor children would *almost* be allowed to eat dinner rather than spend the rest of the night correcting their one mistake, over and over.

So yes, Giff M.E. Huggs got *a little* upset when he wanted something and couldn't have it. Especially when he *almost* had his hands on it.

Like now.

Huggs speed-paced back to his desk, focused on only one thing.

Bratty children.

The thing that got in his way.

Annoying twins.

The ones who had *almost-ed* him.

Nobody gets the better of me.

Huggs tapped an invisible touch pad on the surface of his desk and zoomed in on a blurry picture of a family, a mother, father, and twin children.

He zoomed closer on the twins, fingers trembling.

Especially not them.

If it weren't for those two, he would be busy planning his next acquisition, not hiding in a dark room, speed-pacing, licking his wounds.

Max and Min Wengrod.

Horrible children, with horrible parents that almost surely spoil them.

He growled and tapped again, bringing up a satellite image of a small, shabby home in Los Angeles. In the poorly maintained front yard (so overgrown it was obvious even from orbit, Huggs noted with disdain), he saw the outlines of two small spaceships parked on the lawn.

"There they are. . . . Look at that." Huggs leaned forward. "Are you looking at this?"

"I'm looking at it," a disembodied voice echoed out

from a speaker imbedded in the wall. "I was also there," the voice added, sounding a little bitter. "If you recall."

The voice, belonging to an AI program named House, was, indeed, a little bitter. GloboTech had been using House as a corporate spy in the Wengrod house, until its cover was blown and the Wengrods got the better of it.

"I do recall," Huggs said through clenched teeth, "how you fumbled everything, right at the finish line. When we were SO CLOSE!"

The voice went silent.

Huggs tapped at the touch pad. Through hazy black-and-green night vision, he watched small, odd-sized shapes shuttle between the house and the ships, some on four legs, some on one.

Suddenly, an intense flash flooded the scene—reflecting off that shiny eggshell Huggs called a head—and only one ship remained, cat-shaped.

Huggs tapped again and pulled up a cluster of satellite images showing the curved surface of Earth, dark and cloud-covered. A second flash of light lit the clouds below.

The camera centered on the flash and refocused on the ship as it burst through the clouds, escaping Earth's atmosphere at impossible speeds, leaving a quickly fading trace of billowing smoke.

The sight of the ship leaving orbit triggered a new

level of Huggs rage. He shouted toward his wall speakers.

"HOW COULD YOU LET THEM GET AWAY?"

Huggs kicked away from the desk, knocking it over with a thundering crash.

PFFPPLPLLPT!

The pug yelped and farted—er, yarted—scrambling to a safer distance on stubby legs.

"How did this go so wrong, House?" Huggs resumed speed-pacing, trying to regain some composure. He went through his routine. *Heel-toe. Heel-toe. Breathe out the heat. Breathe in the sweet. . . .*

"Is that a rhetorical question, sir?"

"It's a *question* question, House." *Heel-toe. Heel-toe. Breathe out the pain. Breathe in the gain. . . .*

"Actually, I would argue that many things went quite right," House sniffed. "Granted, we did not capture the Singularity Chip, or the plans to create one, and true, both ships were able to leave Earth. . . ."

"But, House—" Huggs sucked down his rage, hopping in place like a poorly proportioned frog. "Were those . . . were they not . . . in fact . . . THE ONLY THINGS THAT MATTERED?!"

The twins Max and Min Wengrod—not to mention Max's kittens and Min's robots—had managed to keep House, Huggs, and GloboTech from taking control of the Singularity Chip invented by the Wengrod parents. The

Singularity Chip was one of a kind—worth more than all other technology in the solar system, combined.

Huggs wanted the chip.

"If I may," House said, taking control of the screen. The view zoomed back to a close-up of the surveillance video of the house.

Huggs pinched the bridge of his nose, flopping back down into his chair. "Go on."

House cycled through images of the Wengrod property. "I suggest we focus on what we learned and use that to move forward. By going back. Return to the scene of the crime. Ground zero, the Wengrod home. We need eyes on the creators if we want the chip."

Huggs stared. "You're right. We need to know what's going on. We need you to get back into that house. With the . . . Snodgrods? Hogdogs? Wengrods?"

House crackled. "Unfortunately, it can't be me this time. The Wengrods . . . er, deleted me. I've been erased from their systems entirely. Utterly firewalled."

"So you're useless?" Huggs raised an eyebrow.

"Temporarily." House sounded defeated.

"Fine." Huggs eyed the video feed. "We'll use the Roachbot."

"The top secret surveillance robot you're developing for the CIA?" House pulled up a series of classified GloboTech schedules and blueprints. "It appears the prototype is still weeks from being completed."

"Come up with a better idea, House. Until then, seeing as you've been . . . evicted, this is the best plan for infiltrating that shabby shack."

The speakers crackled again. "Affirmative."

As the AI logged out, the walls switched back to an image of the cat ship leaving the solar system.

Huggs reached down into the shadows and picked up his small, stinky companion. He scratched the pug's chin folds as he stared at the stars on the screen in front of him, considering his options:

. . . *get control of that chip* . . .

. . . *fill a galaxy-sized Puggy Bank, while you're at it* . . .

. . . *and show those snotty kids they don't want to mess with Huggs* . . .

The pug gave Huggs's cheek a lick and squeaked out the tiniest toot.

.

.

.

PFFFFFFFT!